SNEAK THIEF

SNEAK THIEF

FAITH HARKEY

ALFRED A. KNOPF · NEW YORK

THIS IS A BORZOI BOOK PUBLISHED BY ALFRED A. KNOPF

All rights reserved. Published in the United States by Alfred A. Knopf, an imprint of Random House Children's Books, a division of Penguin Random House LLC, New York.

Knopf, Borzoi Books, and the colophon are registered trademarks of Penguin Random House LLC.

Visit us on the Web! rhcbooks.com

Educators and librarians, for a variety of teaching tools, visit us at RHTeachersLibrarians.com

Library of Congress Cataloging-in-Publication Data is available upon request.
ISBN 978-1-5247-1747-6 (trade) — ISBN 978-1-5247-1748-3 (lib. bdg.) — ISBN 978-1-5247-1749-0 (ebook)

The text of this book is set in 12.25-point Goudy.
Interior design by Jaclyn Whalen

Printed in the United States of America
March 2018
10 9 8 7 6 5 4 3 2 1

First Edition

For Drew—
my special, crazy friend

WANTED

My name is Belle Cantrell, but you can call me Hush.

I'm what you'd call a sneak thief.

You say you don't know what that is? Look here. One morning, there was me, going into Sass Foods. I walked right up to the counter and asked the cashier where I might find the AA batteries. While she was busy spinning out her reply, telling me up this aisle, right at the end, look underneath the flashlight display, I reached out my hand and snuck a packet of playing cards off the shelf in front of me. Cool as you please, I slid the cards into my pocket, thanked the lady kindly, and wished her a fine day. Then I left the store, strolling all casual-like.

Simple, see?

Though it turns out I am more than *just* a filch and a delinquent. How, you want to know? All right, but the story's kind of knotty.

We'll start on that same day, just a short time later, when I took myself to the laundrymat. Nina, my ma, had sent me with a fistful of change, a pillowcase of stank clothes, and orders not to be home before six. She was having guests, she'd told me, and she wouldn't have me mooning around, staring after her with my dumb cow eyes.

I didn't think I had cow eyes, dumb or otherwise. But I obliged her, pleased for any excuse to get gone from broken-down old 'Bagoville, the trailer park where I lived. Nina didn't much like it when I went to town. She didn't want me anywhere near the nibs, her name for the goody-goodies in town. But she couldn't have it both ways. Either I stayed or I went, and if I went, I went where I wanted. And what I wanted was *out*, past the chain-link limits of my life, away from the field where my people kept company with rusted-out cars, cast-off refrigerators, and the tractor on its side.

It was a real relief to get away, too, because even though there was *some* thieving a person could do from one's kin, too much too often would get you caught—like the time I got busted for five-fingering my grown cousin Sheena's pink lipstick. After that—plus the time they found another cousin's Sashay perfume in my stash—the family watched too close for me to do any real borrowing.

I reckon what I'm shaping up to tell you is that, by age nine, I had discovered a certain truth about myself: I had to thieve. I called it my *loco* because it came over me like a crazy fit, and I couldn't think straight until it was done. But it was also like a train, rolling along so fast, so heavy and wild, a Hercules couldn't stop it if he tried. Once or twice, I did try to halt that train. There was me, standing on that track, all shakin' and trying to stand my ground, feeling like I was gonna die, the train coming, the train coming—and in the end, it only mashed me down flat, and I ended up stealing the hairbrush or whatnot anyway.

And so these trips into town were more dire than pink lipstick, more mesmerizing than Sashay perfume. After only my first hour, in the pockets of my first daddy's jacket, I had my pack of cards, a set of measuring spoons, and a tube of butt-cheek ointment. I didn't know what I'd do with those last two things—truth to tell, it didn't much matter—but I thought I might use the cards to teach myself, what's it called, sleight of hand. And with that, I might step up my sneak-thieving game.

The laundrymat was a yellow building next to a lady hairdresser's. It had seven washers, six dryers, and a big sink for hand washing. Just now, there was a girl leaning over that sink, watching—as far as I could tell—the slow dripping of a leak from the faucet.

"If you take a picture, it'll last longer," I said to her.

The girl turned around. She had big blue eyes, glasses, and a pimple right in the middle of her forehead. Her crayon-yellow hair was tied in a tail held together by a strand of twine.

"What's that mean?" she asked me.

I started to reply but realized, "I don't know. Nina says it."

"Who's Nina?"

"My mama."

"Oh." She waited for a few seconds, as if she wanted me to say something else. When I didn't, she left to go check on her laundry.

Me, I headed for my favorite washing machine. It was an old one—easier to scam—and sat in the back, harder for the attendant to see. I snuck a broken fork out of my pocket. All but one of the prongs was snapped off. Slipping it into the sweet spot which only I knew, I jiggled the fork until the machine clicked inside itself. The faceplate now read WASH.

I opened the door and started shoving in my clothes.

"I think that's stealing," said a voice.

I turned around to find the yellow-haired girl blinking at me.

"I'm sure it is," I told her. "But it ain't hurting nothin'."

Her eyebrows crinkled. "It's hurting Miz Buchanan. She's the owner."

"Huh." Thinking I'd better cover my tracks, I lied. "I didn't know."

"Yeah. Sometimes it's hard to know." The girl gave me an understanding smile.

I waited for her to go away so I could get back to my filching.

Instead, she told me, "I'm Desiree."

4

"Okay," I said.

"What's your name?"

"Uh. Hush." Would she *ever* get gone?

Desiree reached into her pocket and brought out a wrapped candy. She broke off half and handed it to me.

I took the candy. Only a fool would turn away free food.

As she chewed on her half, she mused, "I used to know somebody called Hush. How'd you come by a name like that?"

I shrugged as if I didn't know. But I did. It was one of Nina's jokes. She said I'd chattered so much as a young'un that "Hush!" was all she'd ever seemed to say to me. She told me I was lucky she didn't decide to call me Slap Upside the Head. I never thought it was a very funny joke.

"How'd you come by a name like Desiree?" I flung back at the girl.

"It means *wanted*," she replied. "My ma picked it."

For some reason, that made my throat go tight.

After a second, she added, "I've seen you around. I think you might be my age. Are you? I'm twelve."

"Uh-huh. Twelve," I agreed.

"That *was* you, then!"

What was me? I wondered.

Desiree glanced at the tumbling laundry in a nearby machine. "Mine's still got ten minutes. Want to take a walk?"

"Um. No."

"Oh, come on." She tugged at my arm.

5

"Stop pulling on me, girl!" I yanked my arm back. "I don't want no walk. It's hot out there."

She slow-slid her foot forward and tapped the toe of my shoe. "I do remember you from school. I'm sure of it. You were in Miss Bonnet's class for a while."

It could be. I never troubled to remember the faces of the goody-goodies.

I moved my foot away from her fancy red shoe. "So?"

"They had to take the class picture three times because you kept ducking down."

"I don't like my picture taken."

She slid her foot forward again. Tapped me again. After a second, she added, "You're always alone." Tap-tap. "Every time I see you."

I only barely kept myself from kicking her. "SO?"

"Nobody likes to be alone."

"I do."

She looked at me so long and so hard it gave me the fidgets.

Finally, she said, "I think you need a friend."

Friend. My breath caught at the peril and magic in the word. As far as I knew, there were two kinds of friends in the world. The kind that used you while they could and disappeared when they were done, and the sort from movies, where two people were nice and helped each other, which looked all great and good, but never happened in real life.

"And *you* aim to be *my* friend." I said it singsong, like a taunt.

"I think I do," Desiree replied. "And I think maybe you aim to be my friend, too. You did talk to *me* first."

"Only because I meant to poke at you!"

She clearly didn't believe it.

"Throw off the harness, Hush!" She gave a little jump. "Aren't you curious what might happen if you did?"

I was all ready to say *No,* and even, *Harness this, you crazy goody-good,* when something settled over me. It came with a word, in a Voice that wasn't my own.

Try, it said.

I'd heard the Voice before. More than once, its advice had kept me out of trouble. Meanwhile, the times I ignored it usually turned out poorly. I tried to think of a good reason to refuse it now.

Desiree took my silence for agreement. She'd dragged me halfway out the door before I thought to complain. "Hold up! I ain't even started my laundry yet!"

I raced back, regretfully dropped in Nina's quarters, and— surprising even myself—joined up with Desiree for that walk.

7

2

GOODY

As we passed the hairdresser's next door, Desiree turned her face to the sky. "The summer solstice is almost here, so there couldn't be much more sunlight. Plus all those cumulus clouds daydreaming their way across the sky. It's a right pretty day, isn't it?"

What kind of stupid person gets all stirred up over clouds? I wondered. But as I gazed at her, I realized, *No, that's not the look of stupid. It's the look of* free.

She saw me staring at her. "I get caught up, sometimes. That's what my ma calls it when things are so beautiful, you drift away."

We kept on walking, past the drugstore and real-estate office. Then came the credit union—which had me wondering if money ever got left lying around in there and, if so, how I might filch some.

Desiree came to a stop at the Veterans' Garden, which

was a green spot with two benches, a flag, and a metal plaque with a list of names.

"My great-granddad's name is on here." She pointed to the words CAPTAIN JOHN ORR. "He was mayor, after he came back from the war."

"Your people have been in Sass a long time, huh?" I asked her.

She nodded. "How long have yours been here?"

"Oh, they ain't," I replied. "I live outside of town, just past the 'Welcome to Sass, Georgia' sign."

It was a dopey sign, too, in the shape of the Rural News Network Building. Every couple of months somebody came to repaint the population figure. Last week it was 842.

I could see her thinking that over. "So now you go to school in Pitney?"

"No. I'm homeschooled." That was Nina's lie, not mine, and I didn't like it much. Truth is, Nina had forbidden me to go back to school after a teacher's assistant—a little old lady with watery blue eyes—showed up at our door asking if she might tutor me some. She saw I'd been struggling. It was the nicest thing anyone had ever tried to do for me, but Nina just called it interfering.

"You must be smart," Desiree told me. "I woolgather too much for home study."

A flash of movement caught my eye—and Desiree's,

too, it seemed. All at once, she was making a sound like *Awwwww!* and running toward a man on a horse.

No. Not a man on a horse. A *policeman* on a horse.

"Sheriff!" Desiree called out.

Sheriff? Oh, Lordy.

Even with all my sneak thieving, I'd never actually been busted for anything. But that was partly because I knew when to get gone. Like now.

"Oh, she looks so fine, Sheriff!" To the horse, Desiree said, "Don't you, Miss Porter? Don't you look fancy in your promenade getup? Hush, come see!"

The sheriff turned my way. It was too late to run. I'd just have to put on my Upstanding Citizen face.

"That sure is a fine horse!" I wore my best nib grin, lots of teeth and glistening with gladness. "What's her name?"

"Miss Porter. Like Desiree just said," the sheriff growled. "What's *your* name?"

I was deciding what name to use when Desiree told him that I was called Hush. *And* that I was homeschooled. *And* that I lived just outside of town.

"Is that so?" he asked. "Which school system would that—"

His radio squawked. He reached for an earpiece and set it in his ear. "Thrasher here. Okay, JoBeth. I'm on it."

Turning back to Desiree and me, he said, "Got to run. Y'all be safe." Then, with one final frown made special for me, he departed.

10

"Isn't she a wonderful horse!" Desiree exclaimed as the man rode off.

"Real good," I muttered, wondering just how much trouble this little "walk" was going to make for me.

"And she didn't seem at all shy around you, which horses sometimes do around strangers," she babbled. "I know, because I'm going to be a horse witch."

That was so peculiar, it took me back a step. "A what?"

"You know. The wildish folk who run the horses all night and leave their manes braided in the morning."

"Ain't that a fable?" I asked.

"Uh-uh! I saw one once! She was wispy and thin, with twigs in her hair. I *was* gonna be scared, but the horses loved her *so* much. Folks call horse witching a torment, but that's just because they don't understand. A horse loves to run! It's what they're made for!" She squinched her shoulders with the excitement of it, but when I kept on looking mystified, her voice went a little glum. "You do think I'm addled."

I wanted to tell her it was the addled-est thing I ever heard of, the idea of going around with sticks in her hair, riding bareback at midnight, makin' like a haint. But I didn't.

"I think . . ." I chewed on my tongue for a time. "I think it must be nice to want something."

"What do you mean? Are you telling me there's nothing you want?"

I shook my head.

11

"Not one thing in all of creation?"

"Nope," I denied, though something I might *maybe* want did start bubbling up in my head. I shoved it right back down. One thing life had taught me was that hoping *hurt*.

"You do too want something!" she sang, then leaned in to jab her elbow in my side. "I can tell! Fess up!"

I looked away. "Oh yeah? What do you think I want?"

She stood square in front of me and set her hands on my shoulders. Leaning in, she peered into my eyes like she was searching for something. "You want"—she peered some more and even pushed up one of my eyelids—"to have dinner at my house tonight!"

I jerked my chin back. "I do?"

"Uh-huh." She said it with all the confidence in the world. "Think your ma will let you? You can use our phone if you need to call her."

My head swam. Never once, in all my born days, had I been invited to do anything other than leave. "Naw, I don't need to call her."

"All right!" Her smile was so bright, she made the sun seem a little dim. "Come help me bag up my laundry so I can run and tell my ma to set an extra place for supper! After your clothes are dry, I'll come back and we can walk to my place!"

Like I said, only a fool turns down free food.

———

A wood shingle hung under the mailbox in front of Desiree's house. In the middle it said ORR. Burned into each of the corners was a name: Jimmy, Didi, Martin, Becky.

Desiree saw me looking at it. "They used to call me Didi when I was little." She made a face.

"But you like Desiree better?" I asked.

"Don't you?"

"I think they're both fine," I replied.

She laughed. "You don't get riled up about much, do you?"

That took me by surprise. It seemed to me like I got riled up about *everything*, that my feelings were huger than my body and one day I'd pop like a salamander squeezed under a tire.

"I do. Sometimes," I said.

The inside of Desiree's house was so big and fine, it shamed me. It wasn't just that there were real sofas for sitting and tables with candles and drink coasters, but there were spaces for walking between those tables and sofas, too, so wide that a body could lay down and take a nap on that clean floor. The fabrics of the curtains and the pillows were a friendly patchwork of denims and whites with hearts sewn in, in places. But despite all the finery, there was plenty of good mess. Portrait pictures and homegrown artwork hung on the walls, a stack of school papers spread across a table— and my fingers itched at the sight of an oh-so-soft blanket thrown over the arm of a chair.

The next thing that hit me was the smell of real food. Not box or bag food microwaved to dingnation, but the kind that got chopped on a counter and stirred in a pot. It was the sort of food they served at the charity luncheon at the church down the road from 'Bagoville.

"Didi, honey? Is that you?" a lady called.

"It's *Desiree*, Ma," she replied through gritted teeth. Then she whispered to me, "She refuses to learn."

A woman, wide as she was tall, burst out of the kitchen, her face pink with the heat of cooking. "And you're Hush! Introduce me to Hush, Di—siree." She winked at me.

"Seems you already figured out who she is, Ma." Desiree rolled her eyes, but in a way that let us know she was funnin'. "Hush, this is my ma, Becky. Ma, this is Hush, uh"—she looked at me—"I don't remember your last name."

I quick made one up. "Sikes."

"Hush Sikes," she finished.

Becky reached out a warm hand and gave me a squeeze on the arm. "Welcome, sugar. What'll you have to drink? We've got peach lemonade, water, milk, and"—she made like she was sticking a finger down her throat and fake-gagged—"rice milk."

"That's mine," Desiree told me. "Too healthy for *some* people."

"Too *weird*, you mean," Ma Orr corrected.

"I'll, uh, I'll try some of that weird milk," I said.

I could tell by Desiree's glad expression that I'd done right.

"At least let me heat it up and put a little cinnamon in," Becky pleaded.

"Sure," I agreed.

"Come help your mama," the mama said.

Desiree tugged the pillowcase of laundry out of my hand and set it on the floor. I'd forgot I even had it. "I'll be right back. You can sit."

While she was gone, I circled the living room, which was bigger than I thought because it turned a dogleg on the far side. Another white sofa, but this part of the room had a fine red carpet on the floor and a number of bookshelves, all of them full. In one corner, some glass trinkets shone in a glass case.

I couldn't ever imagine living in a place like that, but part of me did start to marvel. *I got invited here, like a real person. Nobody knows I'm a sneak thief. They think I'm a plain and normal girl.*

If I kept my corners up, I might get invited here *again*. Get offered something to drink and a place to sit *again*. Maybe just for a time, I could forget about my ramshackle old Winnebago house—and whatever slur Nina would throw at me next.

That's when my loco struck me—hit-me-on-the-head, grind-me-into-the-dust irresistible strong. I was gonna steal something, probably more than one something, and there was nothing I could do about it.

Yes, there was! I realized. There was! I could run off right then and steal a football out of the neighbor's yard! Maybe I'd never be able to show my face at the Orrs' again, but at least Desiree would only have hurt feelings, rather than knowing I was a sneak thief, and truly despising me.

I bolted for the door—

—And careened right into Desiree.

"Dog my cats, Hush!" Some speckled milk dribbled out of the glass she carried and onto her shirt. "Are you all right?"

"I'm—fine. Sorry. Sorry," I said. "I was gonna find you, but I got turned around, is all."

She gave the room a puzzled look. "Huh. Well, here's your milk." She handed me the glass. "Let me get a rag to sop this up, then I'll show you my room."

This time, she went and came so fast I didn't have time to slip off.

Desiree's room was papered with pictures of two things: horses and weather. There was a giant wave striking a lighthouse, the curving funnel of a tornado in the middle of a nearly green sky, a roan-colored horse rearing up, wild-eyed. She also had a pair of binoculars on a desk, a set of shelves full of books and treasures, and a whole closet of things that were hers—which desperately wanted to be mine.

Lordy, I was in trouble.

It wasn't fair! These Orrs really seemed to like me! But *nobody* was gonna invite me *nowhere* if they found out half their jewelry and all their perfume was gone after I left.

"Hey, cheese eater—" A boy stuck his head in the room. He gave me the once-over. "What's Smell Cantrell doing here?"

3

TREASURES

Smell Cantrell.

I'd forgotten—but, dang, did it come back to me in a flash.

It was a while back, right after I'd stole my cousin's Sashay perfume. I'd left for school that morning, which I did roundabouts two to three times a week. The perfume was in my pocket, and I had the idea I'd fancy up before school. I was just twisting off the cap when I heard, "Heads up!" A boy running backward with the aim of catching a football came barreling into me. I fell, the perfume slipped—and I was soaked in what I now understand to be a very stinky *eau du toilet*.

The boy who'd knocked me down was fairly kind. He reached out a hand to help me up, at least. But when the other kids came along and got a whiff of me, let's just say that my face was red, my heart was broken, and my school attendance slipped even more after that day.

Smell Cantrell, they called me.

Now here it was, years later, and the name still had all the sticking power of chewing gum in the hair.

To make matters so much worse, Desiree's ma appeared right behind the boy, saying, "Excuse me, *what?*"

I could tell from Becky's tone that she understood some name-calling was involved and she didn't approve. Problem was, just five minutes before, I'd given *myself* a false name. When they found *that* out, I wouldn't keep hold of their victim-pity for long.

Just then, a rainbow-painted pebble on Desiree's shelf caught my eye. Ooh, I wanted to feel that pebble in my palm, and in my pocket—so bad my belly churned.

"Belle, I mean. Belle Cantrell," the boy said, grinning. "Sorry." Then he hightailed it out of there.

"I'm not done with you, Martin!" Becky called after him. "Whichever one of you girls that was directed at, I'm sorry. He can apologize at dinner."

"That won't be necessary," I said.

Desiree gave me a slantwise look.

Becky pursed her lips. "All right. If you're sure." Then she smiled, said, "Dinner's nearly done," and disappeared down the hall.

"What's Smell Cantrell?" Desiree asked when her ma was gone. Her eyes focused full on me, making it hard to spin a lie.

"Can I hold that rock?" I asked, pointing to the rainbow pebble.

Desiree reached for it and handed it over. She was still waiting on my reply.

I slapped the stone from one palm to the other, getting the feel of it, hoping that might be enough to send my loco away.

"Hush is only my nickname," I explained.

"Oh, I figured that," Desiree said.

"And, uh, Sikes, well, that's kind of a nickname, too."

Desiree gave me a slow, confused nod. "I've never heard of a nickname for a last name."

"My family does it a lot," I told her, which was true. False names were the bread and butter of my bill-dodging, skimmy-scamming relations.

"So, Cantrell is . . . ?" she led me.

"My real last name. My first name is Belle." There. I'd said it. "But call me Hush anyway, if that's all right."

Desiree laughed. "Sure it is! I'm hardly one to begrudge someone whatever name they please. Remember? Didi?"

I couldn't help laughing, too. "Oh yeah! Didi!"

Desiree's eyes drifted to the pebble in my hand, which I was still tossing right, left, right, left.

"If you like that," she said, "you can keep it."

My rock slapping stopped. I swallowed hard. I had to repeat her words in my head to make sense of them: *If you like that, you can keep it.*

"You mean it?"

She nodded.

"Wh-why?" Who was this crazy girl, inviting me to supper, offering me her rock, looking at me straight-on with those friendly blue eyes?

"Why else, you clabberhead?" She shone her smile on me. "'Cause I like you!"

"But you don't know anything about me!" I protested.

"I do too."

My disbelief surely showed on my face.

"You know how horses have instincts? How they can tell right away if someone is kind or cruel?" she asked.

"I . . . didn't know that. But okay, I hear you."

"Sometimes I have instincts about people—and I always, always trust them." She took a sip of her rice milk and came away with a cinnamon mustache. "I think it might be my horse-witch powers coming alive."

"And you have an instinct about me?" When she nodded, I asked, "What's it say?"

"It says"—she seemed to be hunting for the right words—"*This girl is valuable and good and you should help her, Desiree Orr.*"

I almost snorted my milk through my nose. *Valuable!* Talk about missing the mark! "Naw!"

She nodded widely. "It's true. I never lie, because horses are the most honest beings on earth, and I try to follow their example."

———

Dinner was *gumbo*, which was lumps of meat and vegetables in sauce. I'm sure it would have tasted very fine if I could have tasted anything, which I couldn't. I was too occupied with answering Pa Orr's questions *and* wiping the sauce off my shirt *and* the squalling demand inside me that insisted that I **Steal. Something. Now.** So much for the idea that holding Desiree's stone would remedy the loco.

"Do I know your daddy, Hush?" asked Jimmy, Desiree's pa. Like Desiree's ma, he was big and well-rounded. There was crinkles at the corners of his eyes when he smiled.

"Not at this time, sir," I replied. "He don't live here no more."

He nodded with a kindly understanding that made me uneasy. "What'd you say your last name was?"

Desiree answered, "Cantrell."

Becky answered, "Sikes."

Everyone looked at me.

"Can I use the bathroom?" I asked.

"Right around the corner, sugar," Becky replied.

As I was leaving the table, I heard Desiree start explaining about how nickname last names were common in my house. I felt like banging my head against a wall. And then five-fingering the picture that hung on it.

The bathroom was on the far side of that living room dogleg, past the place where the glass do-funnies and all those books lay. With the loco building up the way it was, it took all my strength just to cross the room whilst keeping my hands in my pockets.

But I made it! I did! I made it to the bathroom door! I made it inside! I shut myself in—

—And opened the medicine cabinet.

—And stole a box of floss.

Then I sat down on the toilet and cried.

"You all right, sugar?" a motherly voice called out some time later.

"Yes! I've got the runs!" I replied real loud so no one would come looking for me.

Desiree's brother laughed. Becky shushed him.

After another minute, I wiped my eyes, flushed the toilet, and made like I was washing my hands. I hardly recognized the girl in the mirror. What looked merely skinny and dark in the mirror at home was downright sickly and gaunt under the Orrs' fine lights.

Never in all my born days had I felt so despisable.

On the way back to the table, I pinched a book off one of them shelves and stuck it in my coat.

Martin left the table with a plate of pie and the excuse that he had homework to do. I, myself, knew the face of mischief in the making, however, and didn't believe a word of it. Interestingly, I don't think his daddy did, neither.

"I'll be in there in half an hour to check your math," Jimmy said.

Becky dished out a slice of pie for me and one for Desiree. "Ice cream on top of that?"

"Not me," Desiree said.

"Me neither," I said, making Desiree my bellwether.

Jimmy gave us girls a looking-over. "Not much on TV tonight. How about some treasure maps?"

Desiree bloomed so pretty it made me ache. "Yes, yes! I bet Hush never did one before! Did you?"

I shook my head.

Jimmy went away for what seemed like an age. Now, I know it doesn't make sense, but when he came back, I was so scared he was gonna say something about that missing floss. Why he might have gone looking for floss, right then, I can't tell you. Thankfully, he only dropped a stack of magazines on the table.

"S-so, what's treasure maps?" I asked.

"It's easy." Desiree took four magazines from the stack, setting one out in front of each of her parents, then one for me and one for her. "You find pictures of things you want and you cut 'em out. Then you paste 'em to a board, and—" She looked over at her ma.

Becky handed me a pair of scissors. "And then you just let it go, knowing that what you treasure will come to you."

Opening up my magazine, I said, "So cut out all the things I like? Clothes and cars and whatnot?"

"That's a fine way to do it," Jimmy told me. "Or you could do a map of how you want your life to be. If you want a peaceful life, cut out pictures that make you feel peaceful. If you want to have courage, find things that make you think of bravery."

"What kind of things do you cut out, Jimmy?"

He shrugged. "Depends. Used to be that I was angry a lot of the time. I didn't like that about myself, so I cut out pictures that made me feel calm and free." He pointed to a magazine cover where a dolphin leapt from the sea. It was true. That critter did look so wild and free, I imagined no loco could *ever* get hold of him.

I looked up at Jimmy and nodded to show I understood.

He went on, "Speaking for myself, I find it's easier to change once I know what I want to change *into*. Making a treasure map helps me figure that out."

That seemed to be more than enough instruction for everyone else, because a quiet fell over the room, with only the sounds of page flipping and paper cutting.

I considered the first page of my magazine. It showed a lady smiling at a lipstick. She wore a pearl necklace and a diamond clip in her hair. I thought, given the chance, I might steal that lipstick, but as for the other two, a body was sure to get caught pilfering things so refined.

The next few pages were mostly words, the articles in

the magazines. But then I flipped over to something else, an ad that caught my eye. A girl sat on top of a giant cereal box, her legs a-swinging over the side. There were clouds all around her, as if the girl and the box were floating in the sky. It was a head shaker and an eye roller for sure, all of it, except for one thing. Underneath the girl's dangling feet were the words SHE KNOWS LIFE IS MEANT TO BE MAGICAL.

I stared at those words for a long time. At first, they made me think of Desiree, because in a way there did seem to be a certain sort of magic flitting round her. But I read the words again, and I realized, no, it wasn't for Desiree that those words were written. Somehow, they were written for me.

She knows life is meant to be magical.

"Something struck your fancy, Hush?" Jimmy's voice busted in from the world outside.

"Uh," I said. "Maybe."

Desiree leaned over and looked at what I'd found there. "The words, right?" she asked. "Not the picture, but the words?"

How had she known?

"They're good. You should cut them out," she told me.

I looked at Becky, then at Jimmy.

"Don't look at us, girl," Becky laughed. "*You've* got the scissors!"

So I cut out those words. And in no time at all, I had also cut out a picture of a flying bird, two little girls holding hands, and a lady sleeping in a bed so restful-like she was grinning in her sleep. After a time, a bottle of glue got passed around the table, and I stuck my pictures to a heavy paper they gave me.

"And that's what you call a treasure map?" I asked, holding my paper out so I could see it.

Desiree held up hers next to mine. It was far prettier than my page, with more pictures and more words, and it was very likeable. But I decided that, as treasure maps went, if I had to choose one, I'd still choose my own.

"Now you have to put it someplace safe," Desiree explained. "Then, after a while, take it out and see if your treasures have appeared."

It was nearly eight p.m. when Becky offered to drive me home.

Desiree took a ring of keys off a hook in the hall and tossed them to her mama. "I'll come!" Turning my way, she added, "I want to see where you live!"

Could there be a bigger catastroke? If Desiree saw 'Bagoville—Lordy, if Becky found out I was *from* 'Bagoville— I'd be cut off for good and always.

"I don't need a ride!" I said, hauling my laundry, and my tail, out the door. "Thanks for supper! Bye!"

Outside, I raced down the road and ducked between a couple sheds so the Orrs couldn't find me, even if they had a mind to.

4

'BAGOVILLE

The moon hadn't yet risen, but the stars were starting to shine as I wended my way through town and trees. Twice, I caught the flash of a red light on Cheegee Hill.

I slipped a hand into my jeans pocket, brushed past my carefully folded treasure map, and drew out the rainbow stone Desiree had given me. It was warm from the heat of my body. Shimmering flecks in the rock caught bits of street-light as I turned it over in my palm. I tried not to think of the things in my *jacket* pockets, my stealing pockets, which contained all the day's borrows—including the floss and the book I'd taken from the Orrs, who had been so kind to me. No, I wouldn't think about that, no matter how much my twisty, rebellious stomach reminded me.

A dog barked as I turned down the dirt road to 'Bago-ville, an angry growling followed by the *sprang* of canine body hitting chain-link fence. It crossed my mind, right then, that there weren't no good dogs on my side of town.

Past the doorless, tireless pickup with its array of peeling bumper stickers, I came to my own RV. It was nearly swallowed in shadow—we didn't have streetlights at our end of nowhere.

A cherry ember glowed, and I made out Nina sitting on our front step, smoking a cigarette. As I got closer, I could also make out a fair number of bruises on her arms.

"Thievin' kept you out late," Nina observed.

I ignored that. "What happened to your arms?"

She shrugged.

"Where'd you come by them bruises, Nina?" I didn't really need to ask. Nina's latest boyfriend was a hard man who treated people harsh. In times past, I never felt much moved to say something about it. On most days, he ignored me. And it was her life, right? But for some reason, that night, it got under my skin in a way I couldn't account for.

"Baron got a little rowdy," she replied. "What do you care?"

I dropped the sack of laundry onto the ground between us.

"I care because—" Why did I care? Because a body is justified in standing up when someone hurts their ma? Because I'd had a taste of kindness at the Orr house that night and, truth to tell, I kind of liked it? Oh, how Nina would cackle at that.

Finally, I said, "If he hurts you so bad the police have to come out, who knows what trouble we'll have."

"That's what you have to say for yourself?" She shot up and flung her cigarette into the sparse grass. "A-fearin' the cops will find your stash, and so what if Baron beats your ma bloody, so long as your ugly ass gets fed? Some daughter you are!"

I stammered, but no words came out.

"Tell you what, girlie girl. You're so concerned for yourself, you can just sleep outside tonight!" Nina swung open the motor home door, stomped in, and locked it behind her.

I stared after her for a few seconds. Then, all of a sudden—though I can't say why—the wind flew out of me. My knees fairly buckled, and it was all I could do to get my setter onto one of those steps. I don't think I passed three trembling breaths before the world turned to black.

In time, darkness turned to sleep. I dreamed there was a woman standing over me. Her name was Nina, though she wasn't my mother. She was dark-haired, and her dress was red as valentines. The woman leaned forward and kissed my eyelids, and she said, *Soon you'll see something mighty.*

The moon was high when the hooting of an owl woke me. It took a few seconds to get my bearings. Finding myself asleep, upright, and leaning against our door was peculiar enough. But I had a strange feeling, too, like something was different. Something big. Then I recalled the upscuddle with Nina and figured that must be what was bothering me.

"Irksome woman," I sighed again as I picked the door lock.

I tripped over a pile of clothes on the way in, caught myself, and nearly tripped over another one. Nina was in back, asleep on the bed.

I grabbed a screwdriver from the sink drawer and hunkered down to pry the panel off the space where the radio would have gone in a finer RV. Though it was too dark to see clearly, I knew it like the back of my hand, the little nest I'd built inside, one of five stashes I'd stored around the place. This one was my most private one, where only my best borrows went. Inside it, I set the floss and my treasure map.

Desiree's stone, and the Orrs' book, I decided to keep in my pockets.

I tapped the stash panel back into place with the round end of the screwdriver, and was about to go sock away my measuring spoons and whatnot, when I heard a peculiar sound coming from the bed. It took a second for me to figure out it was Nina.

She lay on her back, her legs kicking at the sheets. Her breath came hard and fast. All at once, she let out a—well, I hardly know what to call it. A wail, I reckon it was. Like a hurt animal, or one caught in a trap. It wasn't a human sound, but rather something that came from a lower place where feelings could swallow you.

I didn't even think what I was doing. I quick-strode to

the bed and climbed in beside her. Reaching out my hand, I found the place where Nina's heart was beating like it was trying to break free. Soft as I could, I rubbed that spot back and forth, back and forth. I did that for a time.

Nina didn't wake as I might have expected, but she quieted down and I thought I had soothed her some.

Twice, while I rested with her, the world flashed red. The walls, the mirror—everything—blazed scarlet, then quietly fell back to darkness. I didn't know what to make of it. I do know that I didn't feel worried. And you'd think I would have, seeing a thing like that.

I laid there for a while longer, just to be sure she was good and truly quieted. Then I checked my other stashes the way I always did, and started folding down the dining table. The bench chair opened out, and the whole thing turned into a bed. It wasn't so uncomfortable as you might imagine.

My blanket had gone missing, but I did find a pillow and tucked it under my head.

Back on the bed, Nina started snoring.

It would be a long time before I fell asleep.

Nina's bed was empty when I woke. That was fine by me, not having to cross paths first thing. I ate a few fistfuls of cereal from the box and chased it with a half-full can of soda I found in the fridge. I was musing on what it might be like to go ask Desiree if she wanted to hang out, when I heard voices outside.

I swung open the door. There, sitting on the hood of his truck, twirling his cap on his up-pointed finger, was Nina's boyfriend, Baron. I knew his weaselly face well; he came slinking around often enough. Nina was sitting on the front step again, with a cigarette again. She looked over her shoulder when she heard me behind her.

"Nina, could you come in here?" I asked as nice as I could, feeling it was somehow urgent, now, to get the two of us away from that man.

"No," she said, and turned her attention back to Baron, who was lecturing on his own manliness.

"—So's I took him by the shirt and said, I reckon you're gonna pay me back—outta your *behind*! With interest!"

His knuckles, I noticed, were torn and raw, as if he'd been punishing someone with his fists.

"Nina!" I tried again, though I wasn't sure that flimsy door would do much for us if she did come.

"Hush!" she hissed, waving an angry hand in my direction. "There's a five in the bowl. Go get those things you was moaning you wanted from the drugstore."

Those things I was "moaning" about wanting was toilet paper. Me and my fool priorities.

"Go!" she shouted.

I gave up. Let her do what she wanted. Jacket on, money

in hand, I swung myself sideways out the door so Nina didn't have to inconvenience herself by sliding over an inch.

Feet on the ground and pointed toward town, I heard Baron say, "I know a job just made for a girl like you."

I stopped in my tracks. He wasn't speaking to me. Surely not.

Just keep walking, said the Voice inside me.

But I did turn around. He might decide to punish *me,* if I didn't.

Baron looked at me straight on. "Friend of mine runs a retiree scam. He needs a girl to pretend like she's in trouble, then swindle Pop's money right out of his fat bank account." His grin was a slimy ooze. "You know a thing or two about deceiving to thieve, don't you, Miss Fancy Pants?"

I wasn't even a little interested. Old folks were just about the only people who *didn't* want something from you.

I looked at Nina, waiting for her to laugh it off. To tell Baron she wasn't peddling her daughter out to some greasy hustler. Here's what she said instead:

"Your buddy can put her to work today, if he wants."

There ain't no words for what flew into me, right then. It was like a bomb went off in my chest and shards of me flew into my hands and feet. My whole body shook.

It wasn't because of Baron, though I knew there could be trouble if I defied him. It was the horrible knowing: I truly was nothing more to Nina than dirt under her heels.

I tried to take a step and stumbled. My legs might as well have belonged to a corpse.

Baron fished in his pocket for his phone and said something about calling his friend right now.

The Voice sounded in my head again now, and it was bell-clear: *Get out of here, go!*

Somehow I heeded it.

LOCO

It wasn't me that tore into town that day, but the shell of me, haunted by the feverish ghosts of my ire.

The clock tower chimed as I stood there on Main Street considering my options. I didn't have long to decide. In just the time it took to walk from 'Bagoville, the loco had become nigh intolerable.

The OPEN light flashed on at Beezer's, the drugstore. Decision made.

I sauntered in, fingering the five-dollar bill in my pocket. Toilet paper was too big to pocket, but that didn't trouble me none. It was easier to steal when you were actually buying something, anyway.

I waved to the lady behind the counter. She wished me a good morning and could she help me with anything? I thanked her, but no, I knew where I was headed.

The paper-goods section afforded me a fine view of the

rest of the store. As I made out like I was mulling over one ply or two, I scouted for some promising borrows.

I scooped up the toilet paper with the baby's head on it, then made my way, all browserly, to the gifts department. The candles caught my eye, especially the Moon Wax brand, with all its swirly colors and tasty smells. I lingered over them and made a show of smelling a few. Then the store phone rang. *Yes!*

Knowing I was on a time clock now, I quick rejected the tiny votive candles as too easy and too cheap. I wanted a challenge. I wanted . . . one of them long, fancy stick candles. It wouldn't fit in my outside jacket pocket so good, but it might slide into the inside one fairly well.

Now I heard the cashier woman say, "Let me look in my computer. Hang on."

She wouldn't get more distracted than that. I picked me a candle and slipped it into my jacket. The lady was still busy typing away on her computer, so I grabbed a second stick for good measure.

"Okay, Jenny. I'll put one on hold for you. Bye, now." The woman hung up the phone.

I walked to the counter, plunked down my toilet paper and my money, and was back on the street in under sixty seconds. Easy as pie.

The loco wouldn't let up, though. It had hold of me and it wanted *more*.

I tapped my foot on the sidewalk. I chewed my lip. Down the street, I knew, was the greatest five-finger of all: the ladies' clothes store, Dress Up. I'd peered in its windows many a time but never had the gumption to enter. The goods were too refined, and the owner had beady eyeballs like a hawk's.

Today was the day.

A bell chimed as I entered. A lady standing beside an earbob rack looked up.

She trained those birdy eyebulbs right on me. "Can I help you?"

I smiled. "Thinking of a birthday gift for my ma. I'll just look around."

The lady nodded and went back to hanging jewelry.

As stores go, it wasn't very large. The dress racks were fairly low, too. Old Eagle Eye would see me no matter where I went. But—no—maybe not. Catty-corner to that jewelry display, with its view blocked by a dummy, was a tableful of scarves, all fluttery and beautiful. One of them would mash into my pocket real good.

Slowly, so slowly, I made my way in that direction. I looked at a shirt to one side, a pair of pants on the other. I contemplated price tags and size tags and even held up one skirt against a top, pretending to see if they might match. Finally, I found myself before the scarves.

I reached out my hand—

I relished the feel of those silky fabrics under my fingertips—

I chose a color, green—

—And I shoved that scarf right quick into my jacket.

Then I turned around—and smashed right into the owner.

"Empty your pockets, please," she said.

I stared at a puddle of sunshine around my feet, the light just a-pourin' in through the police station window. Though I was feeling fairly dazed and more than a little numb, it did seem wrong, somehow, that sunshine. A big rain would have been more fitting, or a cold wind, howling through the streets of town.

"Your ma's not answering her phone, Belle," said a lady whose desk sign read *JoBeth Haines, Librarian/Police Dispatcher*. Over her head, a banner read WELCOME TO YOUR PUBLIC LIBRARY! "Can you think of somewhere else I can reach her?"

Sure. She could be running around with Baron Ramey. Good luck finding 'em.

"I'll drive by their place. Be right back." Sheriff Thrasher gave me a warning glance. He looked even sterner without his horse.

I nodded as if I agreed with something he'd said.

"All right. Let's see." The librarian/dispatcher cleared aside a stack of books and set my borrowed things before her. "We've got two candles." She wrote that down. "Package of toilet paper. One scarf." She held the scarf up to the light. "Hmm. Pretty. And a book." Still writing. "A rock. And three dollars and thirty, thirty-one, thirty-two cents."

"That rock and the money, can I keep those?" I asked. "They're mine."

"We'll see," she replied. "Unless I miss my guess, these candles come from Beezer's. That right?"

"Yes, ma'am."

"You steal anything else today?"

"No, ma'am."

JoBeth considered that. "You steal anything else *lately*?"

It was right then, when my brain all by itself started tallying up a list of all the things I'd stolen in the last week, the last month—oh, Lordy—the last year, that my cheeks flashed hot. Shame, like leaden bricks, fell onto me with the memory of every danged borrow. At first they dropped one at a time, and I thought that was bad enough. But when I came to last night, recalling how I couldn't even get through supper without sneak thieving—when I saw Desiree's goodly smile in my mind's eye—that avalanche of shame bricks near demolished me. It took some time to find myself in all that rubble.

I was chewed up. Maybe it was time to wave the white flag and surrender.

Looking at that dispatcher straight on, I said, "You got a pen and paper? I'll write it all down." And, right there at the Sass PD, I made a list of everything I ever stole.

JoBeth's eyes got a little wide when, twenty minutes later, I handed her that page.

"My. Oh, my," she said. Then, in a tone I couldn't quite make out, she added, "That all?"

"All I can remember."

On the desk, the radio squawked. A second later, Sheriff Thrasher's voice said, "JoBeth, there ain't no one here. Unless Cantrell can find someone else to vouch for her, go ahead and call juvie in Ardenville."

My heart stopped. My throat went dry.

"Oh no, ma'am! Please don't send me to juvie!" I knew juvie. My cousin Harlan got sent to juvie and he never was heard from again. And if that wasn't bad enough, something like six weeks after they took him, they came for his mama, too, and *she* disappeared like she'd been swallowed. "I swear I'll—I'll—"

The dispatcher held up a quelling hand. "Understood, Sheriff." Tucking my borrow list into one of the library's yoga magazines, she turned to me. "Miss Cantrell, I could be wrong, but my guts tell me it's not too late for you. So, listen. You've got one chance here. You need to think of some adult, any adult, who will vouch for you. Can you do that?"

I didn't have to think for very long. There was no one. I was just about to say so, and surrender to my terrible fate, when the knowing Voice whispered a name in my mind.

"Belle?" The dispatcher pressed her lips together, waiting and hopeful.

"Yes, ma'am. There might be someone."

She gave a little sigh of relief. "Good. Who?"

"Jimmy Orr."

JoBeth's eyebrows rose. "All right! Do you know his number?" She picked up the phone.

My hopes crashed into that puddle of sunlight at my feet. "N-no. I don't know it."

The librarian/dispatcher waved a hand. "Don't worry. I'll call Sue. She's good friends with Becky."

She made a call to Sue, a call to Becky, and a call to Jimmy. Not five minutes later, Desiree's daddy walked in the PD door. He wore a blue work shirt that said DANDY ANDY'S on the pocket. His eyes were worried but kind.

"Hello, Hush," he said.

"Hello, sir."

"JoBeth, is there someplace Hush and I could talk?"

She pointed us to a hallway on the far side of the library.

I got up to follow Jimmy down the hall, when I remembered something. "Can I have that book?" I jutted my chin in Jimmy's direction. "It's his."

The dispatcher's eyebrows flew up again. "Sure."

We sat in hardback chairs at a little round table. The only other thing in the room was a picture on the wall. It showed a flying duck, the kind with the band around its neck.

I set the book between us. "I stole this from your house."

Jimmy looked at the book for a long time.

"Telling you that probably wasn't the best way to get you on my side," I added.

"Hush," he said, "why did you ask JoBeth to call me?"

"I had to have someone vouch for me," I replied.

He nodded. "I understand that. But why me?"

"I didn't have no one else."

He reached out for the book then, and held it up. "Why did you take this?"

I closed my eyes, swallowed, and admitted, "It's my loco. I couldn't help myself."

"Did you need this book in particular?" he wanted to know.

I shook my head. "No. It just had to be something."

He set the book back down. I was worried he might lash out, but his eyes were still kind.

"Do you know what an addiction is?" Jimmy asked me.

I wasn't sure what it had to do with anything, but I was game. "It's when you can't stop taking drugs."

"That's one kind," he agreed. "But there's others. Anytime a person can't stop doing something, that's what you call an addiction."

I didn't have to cogitate for long before I realized what he was getting at. "I think . . . I might be addicted to sneak thieving."

He nodded. "I think you might, too."

It was too terrible and too wonderful, all at once, to have a name for what I'd done. *An addiction.* I was more ashamed than ever, but the relief of having spoke it out loud made my eyes brim with tears.

"I swear I tried not to take your book, Jimmy!" I cried. "I took your floss, too!"

"Okay," he said softly after I was done with my lament. Then he sighed. "Okay, Hush. Wait here. I'll be right back."

I heard Jimmy's voice, and JoBeth's, as they talked something over. In about ten minutes, Jimmy walked back in.

Setting his back against the door frame, he said, "All right, Hush. Here's what's going to happen."

I took a deep breath.

"After you go home tonight—" he began.

"No! I'm sorry, but no! I can't go home tonight, sir!" I was grateful that Jimmy had come, and I wanted very much for the Orrs to like me, but no matter what, I could not, would not go home only to have Baron Ramey cart me off to be a con man's helper.

Jimmy paused, but he didn't blink. "How come?"

I didn't know what to say or how to say it, so I just shut up.

"I want to help you, Hush, but you've got to help me," he said. "Tell me *something*. Tell me the smallest bit."

I set my hands on the table and looked at them, hard. They weren't a grown person's hands, no matter how much I sometimes imagined they were. Truth to tell, under the harsh PD lights, those hands looked downright small. They could sneak-thieve, but what else were they good for?

I did need help.

"I steal things, Jimmy," I said.

"I know it," he replied.

"But that's all I do. I don't want to trick old people out of their money and leave them broke."

His brow wrinkled. "I don't quite follow you."

It took me a minute to say this last part: "My mother wants to send me to a hustler, to help him run his scam."

He opened his mouth and shut it again before he finally spoke. "I understand you now. Stay put. I'll be back in a while."

This time, I heard Jimmy and JoBeth talking, plus the sheriff, too. For most of it, I couldn't make out their words, but once I did hear Sheriff Thrasher say, "If that woman ain't got a larceny record longer than my arm!" Not long after that, JoBeth peeked in, smiled at me, then shut the door. I couldn't hear anything after that.

The minutes ticked by. At what I reckoned was the thirty-minute mark, JoBeth brought me a soda and a sandwich in a take-out box. Another half hour later, I'd eaten maybe three bites and I was still alone.

Finally, though, the door opened and Jimmy came back in.

He sat down and took his own deep breath. "There's an offer on the table, Hush. Sheriff Thrasher okayed it, and I think it's a good plan. You listen and tell me what you think, all right?"

"Yessir."

"I know a lady in town, her name's Mabel Tromp—sorry, Mabel Holt. She got remarried. Anyhow, she runs a plant business," he explained, "and she could use an extra hand around the garden. Plus her husband and her son are away for the summer, so I reckon she'd appreciate a little companionship. I spoke with her just now, told her about you and your situation. She thought she might be willing to have you stay with her for a while. Now, you'd be expected to work four hours each day—"

"I'll do it," I said, eager to not have to go back and face Nina and Baron.

He lifted his hand. "Hold up. That's not all. You've got you a problem, Hush, and you need some help to fix it. So here's what I need you to promise me. Every time you feel your loco, *before* you steal something, I want you to talk to someone. Me or Mabel or JoBeth or whoever. Though I'd recommend that you choose someone other than the shop owner you're thinking of thieving from. That might not go as well." He smiled.

But me, I wasn't smiling. "I don't know if I can promise that." What if there was no one nearby to talk to? What if the train was a-coming down so hard I couldn't think or talk, but only steal?

"Can you promise to try?" Jimmy asked.

I thought about it. "Yes."

"That's good enough for me. But what that means is,

if you do steal something, you still need to come to me or Mabel, so we can try to set things right. Will you do that?"

The very thought of it made my gut clench, but I did manage to tell him, "Yes."

"Now, there's some other rules you'd have to follow."

I nodded, though I couldn't help wondering how I was going to keep track of all this.

"Any guidelines Mabel sets for you, you have to obey." He tapped the table to let me know he was serious. "And you're not to go see your mother, at home or anywhere else. No matter what. If you need something from your house, clothes or what have you, let JoBeth know and the sheriff will get them for you."

"I don't know how Nina will take that, me just up and disappearing," I said.

"You let me and Sheriff Thrasher worry about that," Jimmy rumbled. "This summer, I want you to think real hard about *you*."

I didn't tell him, but I was already thinking hard.

"What about after the summer?" Going back to Nina's after three months gone, and her having all that time to stew in her juices, getting all cross-legged with me? It might be easier just to go back now.

"That'll depend on how you do. And what your mama does. If you do go back, she'll have to clean up her act."

I sighed. There weren't nobody, nowhere who could ever stop Nina from doing what she pleased.

Jimmy sniffed out my doubt. "As of today, a sizable number of very fine people care what happens to you. You're not alone anymore."

I nodded and tried to believe it.

"What other rules?" I asked.

"Not too much else. I want to see you at my house at least once a week for supper. I hope you'll spend a good chunk of your free time with Desiree. She likes you very much, you know."

I'll admit, that made the darkness seem a little brighter.

"Other than that"—he raised up his hands—"maybe try to eat some more of your lunch while you make a list of things you'll need from your house. In a little while, you, me, and JoBeth will get into my truck and head over to Mabel's." His chair creaked as he leaned back. "So, that's the offer. Take all of it or none of it. What do you say?"

"Can I just ask one thing?"

"You bet."

"Is the other choice juvie?"

"Most likely," he replied.

"I just wanted to know."

He dipped his head. "Always good to know your options."

I looked around me, at my hands on the table, at the duck pictured on the wall. I considered the lunch JoBeth brought and the patient expression of the man sitting across from me. I mused on Desiree, some. Baron's job offer came back to me, as did Nina's cold reply. I thought of the chance

I'd taken that morning, stealing from the finest store in town. Any yokel would have known I'd get caught.

I took a deep breath and swallowed it down. "I'd like to take the offer. And not just because the other choice is juvie."

I gave my list to JoBeth, and she promised the sheriff would have my things to me by nightfall. She also gave me my rainbow rock and started to return my money.

"Could the sheriff give that to Nina for me? It's really hers."

JoBeth looked at me sideways.

"I didn't steal it. It's just change from buying toilet paper." I thought for a second. "Maybe he should bring her the TP, too. She's out."

The librarian/dispatcher laughed. "I'll let him know."

Jimmy and JoBeth and I were on our way out the door when I remembered, "Oh, your book, Jimmy! I left it on the table!"

He went back for it, then handed it to me. "Tell you what. You hang on to it."

"Thanks." I couldn't help marveling. Two presents in two days—and considering how awful I'd been! I'd never known the like.

STASH

As we drove toward Mabel Holt's house, something peculiar happened. It was like a bunch of doors got thrown open in my mind and all kinds of mess started spilling out. Memories like crazy! I saw sunrise breaking over busted appliances. Chickens scratching bare dirt. A pile of trash burning on a cold winter morning.

I recalled Nina chasing off the gray-haired lady who'd wanted to help me with my schoolwork. After that came a memory of a sick dog whining outside our 'Bago door. I had tried to give him water, but he'd died anyway.

Then I remembered my first daddy bringing me some broken crayons and paper with printing on the backs. "It's good enough for starting," he'd said. "But I'll try to get you some better colors when I get paid."

I couldn't recollect the day he left, but I remembered how the shadows in our RV turned dank once he was gone.

I recalled the only time my cousin Sheena ever got struck

49

with a fit of generosity. It was my fifth birthday and she gave me a can of co-cola. It was the shiniest, prettiest thing I ever saw, without a dent or a scratch, and it was *mine*!

Can clutched proudly to my chest, I ran past one rusted-out RV, then another. Nooter, the 'Bagoville cat, batted at a piece of broken glass as I toddled by.

I found Nina, my ma, sitting on our retractable step, her back leaning against some feller's front, him whispering something and her laughing deep in her throat.

"Go away," she said as I walked up.

I held up the can. "Open it."

Nina looked at me through half-closed eyes. "You steal that?"

"Sheena give it to me!" I grinned big. "Can't open it."

Nina took the can and popped the top. I reached out. She started to give it to me, then didn't.

"Thirsty?" She passed the co-cola to the man.

"It's mine!" I hollered.

The man made a show of drinking it down and belching when he was done. Then he crumpled the can and dropped it on the ground.

"Ain't nothin' yours till you're paying the bills," Nina said.

I picked up the squashed can. It was dirty now, not pretty at all. Bits of water collected in my eyes.

"You're even uglier when you cry. Git!" Nina pushed at me with her foot.

I stumbled off, my steps made clumsy by a haze of crying.

As I went, I heard the man say, "That one's got a face only a mother could love."

"Not even," Nina snorted.

"Whose is it?"

"It don't matter. Want another smoke?"

I had waited till Sheena drove off in her car, her face all broken up by the spider lines of her shattered windshield.

Her RV door didn't lock, so getting in was easy.

I went to the fridge and took me a new can of co-cola.

I never did open it. Just stuck it in the glove compartment of an abandoned car and went out to admire it, sometimes.

That memory started the shame bricks crashing down on me all over again.

In the world outside my head, Jimmy Orr's truck shuddered as we hit a pothole. A few seconds later, we rolled up to a flower-painted gate.

The doors in my mind shut themselves back up, as if my brain understood I had to set my attention on new things now.

7

TRANSPLANT

I was a woods tromper as a young'un, so I thought I'd seen some plants. But Mabel's garden, dog my cats! Plants on the ground and plants hanging in baskets from the trees. Little plants, big plants, plants with flowers, and plants with fruits. There were even plants running up the sides of other plants!

And me, I didn't know the first thing about caring for them.

"She's gonna show me what I got to do, right?" I asked Jimmy as we walked through a low, open gate. "I mean, I heard you have to water them, but—"

"She'll show you," Jimmy promised.

"I bet you'll have no trouble at all," JoBeth added.

The house was a strange thing—a small wooden building with a bunch of birds painted on the sides. Still more plants hung at the edges of the porch, as well as some of them dangly noise-makers. As we turned a corner, I could see a lady sitting on a bench swing.

She looked up and saw us. "Hey, Jimmy!" Grabbing the swing chain, she pulled herself to standing. "JoBeth!"

Then she turned my way, so I got my first good look at her. She was only a mite taller than me, but she had more meat on her. She wore a plain dress and a friendly smile. Her belly was baby-round, pregnant, though I wasn't enough of a judge to know how close she was to bursting.

She stepped down off the porch. Her feet were bare.

"Are you Belle?" she asked.

I very nearly corrected her, but something in the way she shaped my name made it seem downright . . . pretty. "Yes, ma'am."

She took my hand in both of hers and gave it a shake. "I'm glad you're here, Belle. I'm Mabel."

I didn't know what to say to this lady stranger who I'd be living with for the next three months, so I held my tongue.

"Hush here was concerned that she didn't know much about gardening," Jimmy said. "That won't be a problem, will it?"

"Absolutely not," Mabel answered. "Beginners make the best and fastest learners."

"Mike will be by later with her things," JoBeth told Mabel.

"I ain't got nothing with me," I added, somewhat shamefully.

Mabel waved a hand. "You can borrow something of mine, if the need arises."

I nearly protested—I just swore off borrowing! But then I realized she must have meant it in the sense of a loaner, so I only thanked her and fell quiet again.

We four of us stood around and stared at one another.

"All right!" Jimmy said after the stillness dragged on good and long. "We'll let you ladies get acquainted." Patting my shoulder, he added, "You'll do fine, Hush."

"I'll work real hard," I said. "Jimmy, Miss JoBeth, I know you two was the only thing standing between me and the bad place, so, uh—"

All of a sudden, JoBeth was down on her knees squeezing the dickens out of me. "You just be good, you hear me? You just be good!"

Pressed up against her as I was, with little room for air, I could only mumble. Still, I think she got a notion of my good intentions.

Mabel chit-chatted as she led me inside. "My husband, Tom, and my son, Travis, are off on a road trip—some much-needed bonding, stepfather to stepson. So, it'll be just us girls for the summer."

Her house wasn't anywhere near as fine as the Orrs', but I felt more easeful, as if it wouldn't be such a tragedy if something got spilled. The arms of the sofa were worn, a puff of batting peeping out from one of the cushions. The table was covered in cut-out pictures that looked like they'd been shellacked on. That reminded me of my treasure map—which was still back at the RV. I regretted leaving it, but couldn't help feeling that sending the sheriff to my stash to fetch it might stir up a whole new wasps' nest.

"I've cleared out Travis's room for you, tried to soften things a bit." Mabel brought me to a shut door, which she opened.

She hadn't pulled down all the monster-truck posters papering the walls or the collection of photos on the closet door—mostly of her teenage son and his special girl, unless I missed my guess. But there was a vase of flowers on top of the dresser—I reckoned that hadn't belonged to Travis—and a yellow-green patchwork quilt on the bed. The pillow had the word *Dream* stitched across it.

"Think you'll be all right in here?" Mabel asked. "The dresser's emptied out, so you can use it any way you please."

"It's real good," I told her. I'd never had my own room before, and for sure no one had ever cut flowers for me. Trying to think of some way to show her how fine it was, I set the rainbow rock and Jimmy's book—my book now, I reckoned—on top of the dresser.

"I'm glad." She seemed to mean that. Clearing her throat, she said, "I was hoping to finish up a certain garden project before supper. Feel like giving me a hand?"

"That's why I'm here," I told her.

"Aw, honey. No, it's not." She set her hand on my cheek, which made me feel a little foolish and a little nice all at once.

As for her words, I didn't know what to make of them.

"So, we've got seedlings here," Mabel said, holding up a tray of small plants, each with its own cubby. "And we've got pots and dirt over here." Seated on the ground beside me, she pointed to a bucket of dirt and a stack of plastic pots. "The seedlings grow fast, so it won't be long before their roots get too crowded—which can be bad. Gardeners call it being root-bound. We need to transplant them so they have room to breathe."

"Transplant. Got it," I said.

She smiled. "The trays are meant so you can pop the seedlings right out, like this." She showed me. "Then you take one of the pots, sprinkle in a little soil, then the seedling, then tuck it in." After she made her demonstration, she held up her hands. "If you spend much time here, you'll have permanent dirt under your nails."

I shrugged. "That don't trouble me."

Passing the seedlings my way, she said, "Give it a try?"

So I did. And after a time or two, I got the trick of it. The main thing was not to stick the seedlings in so deep they got in over their heads.

"Do you have a favorite subject in school?" Mabel asked while we worked.

"I don't—I'm homeschooled." It made me mad, how easy Nina's lie came.

"Oh?"

It took some real will to admit, "No. That's just something I say. I don't go to school."

She reached for a small shovel and broke up some chunks in the potting soil. "How long has it been since you went?"

I thought it over. "Couple of years."

"Did you like any subjects back then?"

I popped a seedling from its tray. It was a scraggly one. "I reckon . . . No, no subjects. We went on field trips sometimes. I liked that." Real gingerly, I set the runt into its new pot. "This one time we drove to a place where they take in hurt animals. The cow was the best. Her eyebulbs were poked out, but she'd take greens from your hands, and didn't bite you or nothing."

"You did better than me. If I saw a cow with its eyes poked out, I'd probably burst into tears," Mabel confided.

I shook my head. "They weren't poked out recent. Besides, she seemed to forget all about it. I guess that can happen sometimes." I finished tamping the dirt in around the seedling. "She was a good girl. I do like cows."

As I set the potted plant aside, I said, "Jimmy said you might have more rules for me." She gave me a funny look, so I added, "I only mention it because I don't want to rile you by mistake."

"Hmm. Rules." Mabel wiped her cheek with a dirt-covered

hand, leaving a smear. "I think my big rule is that we be honest with each other. You've done really good with that so far."

"Yeah, I don't know why. I'm a pretty big liar." I thought on how that might have sounded. "I mean, I do lie—I did lie—aw, dingnation, I don't know what I'm trying to say."

"It's okay. I think I understand." She reached for a fresh tray of seedlings. We were making some real good progress. "What about you? Do you have any rules for me?"

I wasn't expecting that. "Huh?"

"Maybe"—she seemed to give it a think—"you don't like yelling. Or you might prefer that I don't go into your room when you're not there. Things like that."

"Oh." I chewed on the question, having never made up any rules before. I transplanted three more plants before I finally said, "I'd like it if you didn't poke fun at me."

She put down her plant and sat up real straight right then. "Belle, you have my word. I hope we will laugh together— a lot. But I will never, ever poke fun at you."

I hung my head down and shut my eyes tight. Let me tell you, I *felt* those words. After a minute, I picked myself up and said, "You have my word, I will be the honestest girl you ever knew. Honest to you, I mean." It seemed a danger to make such claims for everyone else.

"Very honestly put," Mabel noted. "I think I'm ready to call it a day. Will you help me up?"

As I was shifting around, trying to figure out how best to help her, I asked, "When's the baby gonna be born?"

"A little over three months. I've still got a ways to go." She grabbed onto my arm. "I didn't have nearly so much trouble getting around when I was pregnant with Travis."

"I expect you was probably a lot younger then." I gripped under her elbow and heaved.

She laughed. "You're right, I— Oooh!" Her hand whipped around and groped for her back. "Ow! Ow!"

"Are you all right? Did I—" Had I just broken a pregnant lady?

"I'm fine. I get twinges now and then. All this extra weight up front!"

But I wasn't listening anymore. Something queer had caught my eye.

It was akin to a tail. Or a little flag, pale red and rippling. And it stuck to Mabel right at the place where she'd seized up.

"Ssst! Ssst!" She doubled over. "Dangit!"

The tail flashed dark red, then paled again. I didn't know what it was, but it surely didn't belong there. I grabbed it and pulled. The thing came off clean, a-wiggling in my hand. Real quick, I stuffed it in my pocket so I could go back to helping Mabel.

"Oh." She righted herself all at once. "Oh! That's better. *Wow!* That's nice! It usually doesn't pass quite so quickly."

I offered her a hand to steady herself with, but she was doing fine on her own.

"You must have the magic touch," Mabel told me.

She'd meant it as a joke, but as I felt that thing still squirming away in my pocket, I couldn't help wondering if there might be some truth to it.

"Right, yeah," I muttered. "Magic."

WHATSITS

Mabel asked me to excuse her so she could attend to some pregnant-lady business. I grabbed the chance to run off to my new room. And though I did take a second to marvel how I had my own door to close and my own private room to sit in, my real aim was to get a look at that thing in my pocket.

I do confess, as someone who prided myself on my grit, even I was sweating cold. What was this thing? Was it dangerous? I couldn't help recalling a movie I saw on Sheena's TV, where these wormy aliens came down from space and crawled into people's ears and ate holes in their brains.

I drew it out real careful, hoping it was some kind of flummery leech. It was still wiggling, but no, it didn't seem to be a creature, precisely. There wasn't any face to speak of, nor any sign to show which way was up.

"You ain't gonna slither into my ear, are you?" I asked.

As I held it in my palm, it didn't try to get away or bite, though I did notice a slight aching in my skin underneath it.

Just now, it was the pale red color I'd seen at first and last—not the sharp, dark red it had been when Mabel's twinge flared up. I wondered at that, but couldn't make much sense of it.

But the most curious thing—the one that's hardest to put in words—was the way it *felt*. It wasn't . . . dense. Not the way most things you handle are. More like the *notion* of a thing, it felt something like a tickle of air. Or the warmth coming off a stovetop, where it seems to have a certain *touch* sensation to it, even though it's really just the heat.

Mabel's words came back to me then: *magic touch*. The longer I stared at the thing, the harder it was to believe it was quite . . . natural.

After a time, I heard Mabel rattling around in the kitchen. Closing my hand around the whatsit, I went out to ask her if she might have a spare jar. She seemed pleased for the request and offered me not one, but five jars of various sizes. I took the second-smallest one and thanked her. Then I went back to my room, put the thing in the jar, and sealed it in.

It went right on a-rippling.

That night, Mabel and I watched the Rural News Network's *Daily Sum-Up*, which wasn't as terrible as I'd imagined.

"Not too shabby, Kip," Mabel muttered, smiling a little.

"Huh?" I asked.

She blinked. "Oh. The man that owns the RNN, that's my first husband, Kip Tromp, Travis's dad. I was just thinking he's done all right for himself. It's nice."

"Did he used to be a slimy miscreant?" Nina sometimes said that about Sheena's ex-husband.

Mabel's lips twitched. "No, not slimy. I think he just . . . had to leave for a while so he could find his way home."

I was glad that made sense to her, because it sounded like gibberish to me.

After the *Sum-Up*, we clicked off the television and headed to bed.

"Oh, Belle!" Mabel turned away from her door and back toward me. "I didn't even think! Are you used to being tucked in?"

I couldn't help myself. I laughed so hard and so long that tears sprang up in my eyes and rolled down my cheeks. The fit went on for a good while before I finally managed, "Nina? Tuck me in? No, ma'am! I can't say I'm used to that!"

"Ah." She didn't seem to know what to say to my outburst. "All right, then. I just didn't want you to feel neglected."

The word *neglected* rang like a sharp bell in the space between us, leaving an uneasy echo in the air. I knew that was how things were between me and Nina. How could I help knowing?

Finally, I said, "You ain't made me feel neglected, Mabel. Not a whit. Good night."

She gave a smile, though its edges twitched down just a little. "Sweet dreams, Belle."

I went to sleep in my own room, in a bed that didn't double as a dinette. Beside my head, on a little table, the whatsit wriggled in its jar.

My dreams were full of Baron Ramey and his con-man friend. They laughed and twisted my arms and stuffed my pockets with old people's money. All the while, Nina sat on the dinette bed smoking cigarettes, one after the other. Twenty-some whatsits stood out from her chest, wriggling like faceless snakes.

When the sun broke through the blinds, waking me at daybust, I wasn't feeling so good.

Over breakfast, which was fancy eggs on top of English muffins with sop, I said to Mabel, "How would it be if I worked in the garden this afternoon, instead of this morning?"

She waved a hand. "That's no trouble."

I took a bite and mumbled through my food, "I thought I might go into town."

For just a sliver of a second, she froze. "Everything all right?"

"Oh, sure. Just"—look at me, being all honest—"bad dreams."

Mabel reached for the juice pitcher. "Want to talk about them?"

I shook my head. After a quiet minute passed, I asked, "Do I have to?"

"No. I'm just, um, a little concerned." She shrugged. "Maybe I don't need to be. But you look so chewed up this morning, plus you say you had bad dreams. With you wanting to go into town, I thought you might—"

"—Be fixin' to steal something?" I offered.

"—Be struggling," she finished.

"I don't know why I want to go into town," I said. "I just do."

Just then, in the eye of my mind, I saw myself walking into town. I was wearing my first daddy's big, baggy jacket, even though the day was hot. The stores lining Main Street were open, their doors thrown wide. From inside the shops, there came a whispering. It was the voices of all the things that wanted me to steal them.

Maybe *I* didn't know why I wanted to go to town, but my loco did.

I put my head in my hands. *I hate this.* And after a second or two, another fretful thought: *I'm going to juvie, for sure.*

"Belle, can I tell you something about me?" Mabel asked.

"What?" I confess I wasn't lively with interest.

"I used to have a loco, too."

I looked up at her. "Naw."

She nodded earnestly. "Mine was about food. I'd eat and eat and eat, and then throw it all up."

I couldn't help glancing at the fancy food on the table. "How come?"

She leaned back in her chair and gave a half shrug. "It's funny. I don't really know. I mean, at the time, I thought it was because I was afraid to get fat. But now, looking back, that doesn't *really* explain it." She pressed her lips into a flat line. "I did it because I did it. I had a sickness. Like someone who has a cold can't help sneezing, I couldn't help throwing up."

"But you don't do it now," I ventured.

"No."

"So you beat your loco!"

She took a deep breath and blew it out before she replied, "No. *I* never could beat it—"

"But—"

"But *something* did."

"Something, but you don't know what?" I was confused. And vexed. Whatever had helped her, I wanted it, too. *Needed* it desperate-like, so I wouldn't go to juvie. So the Orrs would like me. So—

"Something, but I can't *say* what. It's hard." Mabel looked out the window, thought for a time, then turned back to me. "Did you ever hear a voice in your head, maybe when something bad had happened, and it spoke to you, or it helped you—"

She had my full attention now, by godfrey. "Like a voice that tells you to run away from something bad?"

She nodded real slow. "Like that, yeah."

"I might know what you mean," I told her. "That's what beat your loco? The voice in your head?"

"But it's not just *any* voice. Definitely not *my* voice." She seemed to cast about for more words, but couldn't find them. "Do you—do you know what I mean?"

Most surely I did.

It was the Voice that told me to run from Baron that morning. The one that knew things I couldn't possibly know, and sometimes saved me with its smarts. "You mean the *knowing* Voice."

Mabel hugged her own round belly.

"Yes, that's it." Her whisper carried a shade of wonderment. "The knowing Voice."

After some more gabbing, Mabel and I agreed it might be best if I didn't go to town right then. She did say she thought it would be good for me to get out and have a little fun, though. So we piled into her truck, and she dropped me off at Desiree's house.

On the way out Mabel's door, I'd grabbed my whatsit jar.

Desiree flung open her front door, grabbed me by both shoulders, and cried, "I am SO glad to see you!" giving me a solid shake with every word.

For some reason, I had a notion she was glad to see me.

You know that made me smile some.

"Wait until you see!" Today her yellow hair swept wildly around her face. She wore an orange vest over her clothes. NOAA, it read. When she caught me looking at it, she said, "Oh! My dad got this for me at a government-surplus auction. Isn't it cool?"

Cool was not the first word that sprang to my mind, but I nodded right along. She made it hard not to.

"But that's not what I want to show you! Look!" She strode into the living room, snatched a piece of paper off the table, and held it up so I could see. *Smile for the camera!* it said, and showed a picture of a horse with its face in the camera lens, its teeth bared in a silly grin.

I looked at it for a time. "Uh, I don't know what to make of that."

"Okay!" She took a big gasp of air. "So! The RNN is branching out to other kinds of shows besides news, and one of their ideas is a new reality show called *Horse Dentist*."

"Horse . . . Dentist," I repeated.

"Yes! And they need a couple folks to help soothe the

horses while the dentist works on them—which is about the best training I can think of to become a horse witch! Right? I mean, if I can calm horses around a *dentist,* I won't have any trouble convincing them to ride through thunderstorms and such!"

"And have you maybe been chosen to *be* one of those horse soothers, Desiree?" I ventured.

"I have! I have!"

"Congratulations!" Never say I don't follow a current when the river demands it.

"Thank you!" Then she hugged me and jumped up and down like mad.

And, do you know, I found myself hugging her back and even jumping up and down a little, too.

"So, what's going on with you?" she asked, once her giddiness spun down some. "Are you thirsty? Do you want a drink? Are you hungry? We have food!" She backed into the kitchen, hand still ahold of my sleeve. "Come look in the fridge!"

"All right!" I laughed. "But calm down some! You're making me goosey!"

"Am I being too much?" She rolled her eyes and shook her head, evidently at her own too-muchness. "My ma says I can be. Please"—she petted my arm in long, silly strokes—"relax, have a seat, be my guest."

"Now you're just devilin' me," I observed with a smile.

"Maybe a little. But I will calm down." She took a deep

breath for show. "See? Calm. Now, you want a drink?" She opened the fridge and peered in.

"Yes, please."

While she searched, I got my first gander at the Orrs' kitchen. There were cow potholders and a cow clock. Bovine spoon rests and a bovine cookie jar. The curtains even featured romping cows. I confess, that tickled me almost beyond good sense. And nicer still was how quiet my loco was in the face of all those doodads.

"Oh! Hold up." Looking off toward another part of the house, Desiree shouted, "Ma? Can me and Hush open the punch?"

"Only if you keep it down!" Becky called back.

"She's got a headache," Desiree told me, grabbing a bottle. "This stuff is *so* good. Now, really, tell me all your news. You left so fast the other night, I wondered if you might have got in trouble for being late."

"Oh, that. No. No trouble," I told her. "But . . . truth to tell, I would like to run something by you."

She poured us each a glass of punch and set it on the table. Then she turned a chair backward, straddled it, and said, "Shoot."

I paused to drink in Desiree's fine companionship. Maybe it was silly, considering how we'd only just met, but I was starting to like her so very much.

I must have gazed too long, though, because she cocked her head and said, "Go ahead. Run something by me."

There was nothing to do but to do it. I took out the jar and showed it to her.

"Desiree, what do you think this is?" I asked.

She studied on it for a second. "A mayonnaise jar?"

That surprised me some. "I mean *inside* it."

"Oh. . . ." She took the jar from me and gave it a shake. The whatsit shook right along with it. "Is this a puzzle?"

"No. Look." I took the container back and pointed straight at the pale red rippler.

"I don't . . . um . . . Do you mean that speck there, on the glass?"

"No! I mean the wriggly red thing!"

"Did you catch a bug? Maybe it escaped!" She reached out to check the lid for tightness.

"Desiree!" I cried. "Don't tell me you don't see a weird red thing in there!"

Eyes wide, she shook her head.

"Well, dangit! Now I'm crazy, too!" I grabbed me a chair and flumped down.

Desiree turned her seat to face mine. "Maybe not. Before my granny died, she saw my dead grampa, and nobody else could see him."

"You're just being charitable," I complained.

"I'm not! I really do believe there's things that are real, but we can't see them. Like gravity."

"Yeah, but we can *feel* gravity!" I stamped my foot on the ground. "We can at least agree it's there!"

"Okay, what about"—she tapped her upper lip—"my feelings? If *I'm* happy, you can't see my happiness. You can't feel my happiness in your own heart. But it's real."

"I can see your glad expression, though," I retorted.

"Sure, but anyone who has a ma knows a person can sometimes smile when they're angry."

It took some cogitating, but I finally came around. "So, you do believe me, there's something in this here jar?"

Those sincere eyebulbs of hers! When she dipped her chin *yes*, I knew she meant it.

"But I can't see it," she said. "So you'll have to tell me. What is it? How'd you get it?"

I told her about seeing the whatsit on Mabel's twinging back, and how I'd plucked it off. I told her what it looked like, the faint ache when I held it in my hand, and how it had no openings or closings to speak of.

"Can I hold it?" Desiree asked. "Can you put it in my hand?"

We gave it a try.

"Hush! I think— It's there, isn't it? I think I can feel something!" She closed her eyes. "Like a . . . toothache sort of pain."

"Yeah! Yeah!" I agreed. "Now, wait a minute."

I made like I was taking the whatsit off, but in truth I left it on her palm.

"It's still there," Desiree said. "You didn't take it."

Boy howdy, did I whoop! "It's real! You can feel it and it's real!"

Just then, Becky came into the room, her hand pressed to her temple.

"Hello, Hush," she greeted me with a tight grin. "I'm glad you're here. You're always welcome. But will you please, *please* keep it down?"

"I—I—" I stammered. "Yes. Sorry." I very nearly didn't get the words out, for I had seen something terrible.

"Thank you kindly." Becky opened the freezer, took out an ice bag, and departed again.

"Hush! What's wrong?" Desiree grabbed my shirtsleeve. "You're as pale as moonbeams!"

"Your—your ma gots 'em!"

"Gots what?" she asked, alarmed.

"Whatsits! Three of them! Poking out of her head!"

USEFUL

"Are you sure?" Desiree demanded to know.

"I could see them clear as day!"

"You have to get them off, Hush! You've got to!" She grabbed the front of my shirt and shook me.

I gripped her hands. "You'll have to stop rattling me first!"

She let me go. "Sorry! But you've got to—"

"I know. I will. Where is she?" I went into the hallway and looked around for Becky.

"She's in bed. Come on!" Desiree ran off.

I found her down a hallway I hadn't yet seen. That Orr place sure was big.

"You know . . . ," I said, "I still don't know for sure if the whatsits are bad."

"You don't know they're good, either!" She threw open the door. "Ma, Hush needs to look at you!"

"Look at me, why?" Becky groaned.

The curtains were shut tight, so not a peep of light could

get in. Poor Becky was nothing but a shadowy lump under the covers.

"I—I thought I saw something on you." There. By the letter of the law, that was true.

"Like what?" Desiree's ma pulled down the covers a little. The whatsit tails were deep red, rippling away on her forehead. "Like a bug?"

"Yeah, like that." I got up close to the bed. "Here."

She held out her face as much as the pain would allow. I reached out and, with one sweep, plucked off all three thingies.

"Got it," I told her, stuffing them into my pocket.

"What was it?" Becky asked. But before I could reply, she pushed herself bolt upright. "Hey. My headache's gone."

Desiree gasped.

"Like, gone, gone?" I asked.

Becky nodded. "Gone, gone. That's the strangest thing. Usually they hang on until the small hours of the morning."

"I wonder, Becky," I said. "Do your headaches come and go, or is it one long pain?" I couldn't help thinking of how Becky's whatsits were deep red all the time, but Mabel's only flashed dark when she twinged.

"It's one long pain," she replied. "Twelve or so *hours* of unrelenting pain. Except this time." She shook her head. "I don't even want to question it. I'm just grateful. And to celebrate, I think I'm gonna hop in the shower, throw on some fresh clothes, and put on some sweet tea."

"That's, uh— I'm glad you're feeling better," I told Becky. "I reckon we'll go back to, uh, what we were doing. Sorry to bother you."

"No trouble." Becky stuck her legs out from under the covers and wiggled her toes. "Mm-mm! I do feel good!"

I snatched the mayonnaise jar from the kitchen and raced into Desiree's room. The three whatsits were wriggling like mad in my pocket, and I didn't want them to get loose.

"Did you see that?" Desiree rushed in after me.

"It took away her pain!" I answered, nodding hard and fast.

Once the new whatsits were sealed up, I set the jar on Desiree's dresser and considered it. "What *are* these things?"

Desiree threw herself down in front of her bookcase and started plucking out books, as if the answer might be written in something called *Observing and Recording Weather Patterns*.

I studied the four thingies, all of them now a soft red color. "It's peculiar, how they seem to go deep red when the pain is very bad, but they're sort of pale-ish otherwise."

Desiree snapped shut the volume in her hands, blew out a noisy breath, and said, "I think they're pain imps."

Excited that she might have figured it, I spun around. "What's pain imps?"

"I don't know. I just made it up," she replied. "But don't you think that's what they are?"

I was a mite disappointed, but I pressed on. "Well, what's an imp? It's like a ghost, ain't it?"

She bobbed her head from one side to the other. "More like a sprite. They have mischief."

"Yeah, but don't they also have faces?"

She quirked her lip. "I don't think they *have* to."

It didn't tell us anything, really, but it was a better name than *whatsit*. "All right, then. They're pain imps," I agreed, reaching for the jar again. "Now what?"

Twenty minutes later, we were still puzzling over that question when Becky called from the kitchen, "I'm outta teabags, y'all! Wanna take a drive? I'll buy you both an ice cream at Ham's."

"To town? Uh . . ." I dithered, recalling my talk with Mabel that morning.

"We should go!" Desiree whispered. "You can see if other people have them!" She hitched a thumb at the pain imps.

That *was* an idea. "But you'd stay right with me?"

She gave me a funny look. "It's okay, Hush! I know they're weird, but"—she picked up the jar and gave it a shake—"if they are imps, I don't think they're dangerous. Just a little rascally."

When I kept on looking worried, she promised, "I'll stay right with you."

"All right, then," I said.

But what I was thinking was, *Please, oh, please, let my loco stay down.*

It turned out to be no trouble at all. I didn't even have to go into any stores. Becky dropped us off at Ham's Restaurant with a ten-dollar bill, told us to order what we liked, and promised she'd be back in two shakes.

A string of chimes jangled overhead as we stepped inside.

I'd only ever been inside Ham's once, back when my cousin Harlan was going with a waitress there. This was before Harlan got sent to juvie, of course. The girl had given us some free onion rings, but I only got a couple before Harlan polished them off.

The place was much livelier now, with two waitresses and nearly all the booths full. A lady with a name tag saying SUE walked up to greet us. A pain imp stuck out of her left ear.

"Hey, sugar!" Sue greeted Desiree. "Who's your friend?"

"This is Hush," Desiree told her.

"Well, hey, Hush!" Sue beamed brightly.

"Hey, ma'am."

"Table for two?"

"Yes, please," said Desiree.

Soon as Sue turned her back, I pointed at my ear, then at Sue. *Pain imp,* I mouthed at Desiree.

While Sue was setting down our silverware, Desiree ventured, "Is your ear hurting you, Sue?"

78

Sue put her hand to her left ear. "Was I fiddling with it again? I didn't even know. Yeah. It's swimmer's ear. Seems I get it at least once every summer. Ain't nothin' but a thang. What can I get y'all?"

"Hot fudge sundae, mint ice cream," Desiree said.

I glanced down at a menu on the table. My head fairly swam with all the choices. "Same," I surrendered.

"You got it." Sue gave us another grin and whisked off.

"Dog my cats, Hush! You can't tell me you're crazy now!" Desiree grabbed my hand and squeezed tight. "Does anyone else have them?"

I took a gander.

Oh, Lordy.

Everyone else had them. A pain imp on the crook of the jaw. Another on a knee. A man with so many springing from the back of his head, he almost looked afire. One old lady stirring her coffee had an imp at every joint in both of her hands.

Finally, after lots of careful looking, I did see *one* person who didn't have an imp. It was a baby, asleep in her mama's arms, the next booth over. Her ma had one, though, fluttering on her big toe. *Must have stubbed it,* I reasoned.

Turning back to Desiree, I whisper-shouted, "There's so many! It's awful!"

"Awful? No, no! It's the best thing ever, Hush! Don't you see?" She gave my hand another tight squeeze. "You can fix it! You have a superpower to take away pain!"

I gave a wild, crazy sort of laugh. "Desiree, I can't just walk up to people and say, 'Hey, I see you've got a pain imp. Let me get it off you!' They'd think I was touched!"

"Maybe, maybe not," she said. "But you could be sneaky." She gave a pointed, sideways look just as Sue reappeared and set our ice cream in front of us.

"Sue, you've got something in your hair." Desiree stretched out a hand, then pulled it back. "I don't think I can reach. Hush, can you get it?"

Sue stayed bent over. "Get it, would you, sugar? I've got syrup all over my fingers."

"Uh, yeah." I reached up, grabbed the pain imp, and quick hid my closed hand under the table. "It wasn't much. Just a piece of fluff."

"Thanks anyway. Last thing I'd want is for folks to be calling me Ham's old fluffhead." Sue winked.

"Welcome." I smiled.

As she walked away, Sue stuck her finger in her ear and wiggled it around. "Huh!" she said, sounding pleased.

Desiree's eyes flew wide. "See! That wasn't hard at all!"

"No," I had to agree. "It surely wasn't."

Let me tell you, my first-ever hot fudge sundae with mint ice cream was a mighty right thing. But eating it across the table from the nicest girl I ever met, *and* her gushing all the while about how important and superpowered I was—that amounted to one of the finest days in all my twelve years. I hardly knew what to do with myself.

Becky and Desiree drove me back to Mabel's in time to get my four hours of work done before dark.

"You live with Travis Tromp?" Desiree asked as we pulled into Mabel's driveway.

"Uh, no, I, uh . . ." What could I say? The whole story would take an hour or two plus a scorecard for keeping track.

Becky piped up, "Travis is away with his stepdaddy, so Hush is giving Mabel a hand. Meanwhile, she's learning, like a gardening internship."

I reckoned from that, that Becky knew about the Hush Cantrell rehabilitation plan.

"I didn't know you liked plants!" Desiree said.

"I'm learning to like them," I told her.

"Horses are *very* dependent on plants," she pointed out. "It really is good that we met!"

I muttered that I thought so, too. But something was bothering me. Desiree seemed to be thinking of me as a real friend. It felt unfair to leave her with such a slim sliver of the truth.

Could she still like me if she knew who I really was?

"Um. Me staying with Mabel—" I began. "You're right, Becky. But it's not *just* a gardening internship. There's some . . . things happening at my house. Some troubles. So the sheriff thought I should leave for a while." I wasn't bold enough to admit my thieving.

Desiree frowned, and I thought I was done for.

But what she finally said was, "That's sad. It's so hard to be a person sometimes, isn't it?"

I blew out a big breath. I hadn't scared her off. And, somehow, she'd known just the right words to say.

"Yeah," I agreed. "Real hard."

For a few seconds, the only sound between us was the car's engine.

"Hush, do you have everything?" Ma Orr asked me, though the only thing I'd brought with me was Mabel's jar.

"Got my pants on. Got my shoes," I joked as I opened the door.

"Try to come over again soon." Desiree handed me the imps as I climbed from the car. "We have *important* stuff to talk about." Not so sneakily, she pointed at the jar.

Becky chuckled. "You're a peculiar little thing, Miss Desiree Orr." Then she reached over and gave her daughter a hug and a kiss. "But—ooh!—I love ya."

Mabel was just stepping onto the porch as my friends drove off.

She saw what I was holding. "Couldn't find a use for that jar, after all?"

"No." I grinned. "I did."

———

I kept the jar of imps beside me while I did some weeding. I was fairly sure they weren't going to escape, but it seemed best to keep them close all the same.

"Hey, Mabel," I called.

Mabel, who was maybe thirty paces away, snipping herb leaves, replied, "Mmm?"

Holding up a wrenched-out flower, I asked, "How do you pick which plants you like and which you don't?" I couldn't help wondering what the weeds did wrong.

"I guess there are things in a garden that are useful, and things that are not," she mused. "Part of my job is to grow herbs, so they're useful to me." She waved a hand along the tops of a bunch of basil. "There are some plants that would come in here and multiply so furiously that they'd squeeze the herbs out. And that guy you've got there?"

I showed her the flower.

She nodded. "His roots would strangle the roots of those tomatoes. Tomato—another useful plant, especially when I want spaghetti! So-o . . ." She paused for a time to focus on her work. "So, that strangler plant is what *I'd* call a weed. I'm not saying he's not useful somewhere. I'm sure he is. Just not here."

I had to agree, that did seem like good sense. "It does seem a mite sad, though," I said. "The flower is kind of pretty."

A soft breeze wafted over us, carrying the scent of herbs and flower blossoms. Overhead, a bird crooned.

"Belle?" came Mabel's voice.

"Yeah?" I kept on pulling up weeds.

"We've got plenty of pots and soil. Why don't you plant a couple of your flowers there?"

"Plant the weeds in pots?" I asked.

"Sure. With a good, solid container around them, they can't hurt anything, and you can enjoy them."

I thought it over. "All right, I will."

"And after that," she said, "let's call it a day. I'm hun-gry!"

"I could go for some of that tomato spaghetti." I couldn't help noticing that, since I left Nina's, I was starting to develop quite an appetite.

"Spaghetti it is!" Mabel eased herself up from her chair and wiped her hands on her jeans. "Oh, also, I'm taking a delivery to the hospice up in Pitney tomorrow. It'll be an early morning, but do you feel like giving me a hand?"

I told her I'd be pleased to. Then I found three painted yellow pots, planted my weeds, and wished them a good night.

CRISPY

When Mabel said early, boy howdy, she meant it! We were up at five-thirty, loading boxes onto her pickup at six, and on the road at six-thirty. Pitney was a good piece up the road, so once you included Mabel's pee stops, we didn't get there till almost eight.

It was a plain building, where she parked. Biggish, two stories high, and with a sign out front that said DIGNITY HOSPICE.

"Hospice," I said to Mabel as she snapped off the radio and dropped her keys into her bag. "That's like a restaurant, ain't it?"

She had been about to get out of the truck, but changed her mind. "Oh, Belle. I thought you knew. I wouldn't have brought you here without—" She pressed her lips hard together. "A hospice is where people go to die."

I wasn't too perturbed by that. Folks lived, then they died. "So, it's a hospital?"

She squinched her eyes like she was puzzling something out. "*Sort* of. It's nicer than a hospital. More like a home, but with doctors and nurses." She waited to see what I thought of that.

I didn't think much one way or the other, so I only said, "And they like your herb fixin's here?"

She nodded. "Sometimes sick people have trouble with their skin, so they like my lotions. But I've also got treats in back, cookies and stuff."

"I wouldn't mind if the last thing I did before I died was eat one of your oatmeal raisins!"

"So, you're okay with this?" she asked carefully.

"Sure. Everybody dies someplace."

"Okay, then," she said, opening her door. "But if it gets to be too much, you let me know."

I reckon the best way to describe the hospice was *soft*. The cushy chairs were soft, and the carpet was *real* soft. Soft guitar music twanged in the air. The lady at the front desk had a soft way about her. Even the air, with its smell of lavender, felt soft.

"Missus Mabel Holt!" the lady said gladly, but softly. "How are you?"

"I'm grand, Miss Emony." Mabel smiled. "I'd like you to meet my friend, Belle Cantrell."

"Hey, Miss Emony." I gave a polite wave.

My attention wasn't really on the lady, though. Mabel had just called me her friend! Was I, really? And if I was, maybe having a friend like the ones in movies . . . wasn't such a far-fetched thing, after all.

"I've got all sorts of goodies out in the truck," Mabel told the lady. "Should I just bring them on in?"

"Nuh-uh, *mamacita.*" Emony wagged a finger. "I'll call one of the volunteers to bring the cart around. Will you be stopping in to see Crispy? Should I make y'all some visitor's passes?"

"I think so," Mabel said. "You don't mind if I visit with a neighbor friend of mine, Belle? You can come in or stay out here."

"I'll come." Turning to Emony, I added brightly, "Slap me up one of them visitor passes."

We rode an elevator to the second floor and passed by a number of open doors on the way to Mabel's friend's. I saw what Mabel had meant about the place being like a home. Even when a person was tied to beeping machines, it was common to see them sitting on sofas, maybe with a blanket tucked up around them, maybe even a dog on their lap. I did pass one room where I thought the person—maybe a lady, maybe a man—might already be dead. They laid there real still, with their mouth hung open, so skinny they were practically a skeleton. The only thing that made me think they might be alive was the rippling, pale-ish pain imp that twitched on their belly.

"All right?" Mabel asked when she saw me looking.

"Sure."

She nodded. After another few paces, she stopped in front of a closed door. "He's in here." She knocked.

"Come!" a voice creaked.

"It's me—Mabel." Mabel eased open the door.

Paper flowers sat in vases on the tables, and brightly colored paper chains hung from the ceiling like Christmas tinsel. A poster taped to one wall, written in little-kid print, said GRANPA'S BIG ADVENCHER! above a drawing of a gray-haired man wearing white robes and a yellow halo. Photos—framed, tacked, and taped—took up most of the wall space. One recliner chair was devoted entirely to a pile of toy animals. Another one held a tiny old man so swaddled in blankets he might have been set upon by a swarm of crochet biddies.

The man's eyes got wide. He burst into a toothless grin. "My dear! My favorite neighbor, Mabel!"

"Crispy!" She crossed the room and gave the man a careful hug.

"Who's your young friend?"

I walked up to them. "I'm, uh, Belle, Mister Crispy."

"Oh, just Crispy'll do!" he told me. "And what's a Belle for?"

"Well, she's helping me deliver some treats," Mabel replied.

"And here I thought a bell was for ringing!" Crispy exclaimed with a gleeful slap of the knee.

Sure, it was goofy, but I couldn't help chuckling.

Mabel moved an enormous stuffed bear off a nearby sofa. "Do you want to sit, Belle?" She sat herself down.

While I pulled up a chair, she asked, "How are you, Crispy?"

"Well enough, I reckon," he replied.

Mabel nodded. "And how'd that cupcake work out for your grandson? I know you were worried about him."

"Oh! *Yes!*" Crispy tried to sit a little straighter. "Things came together real good for him! He's working nights to start, but they say if he keeps his corners up, he'll be on the day shift in no time. Thank you for that, Mabel."

"It was no trouble at all, Crispy." Leaning in, she raised an eyebrow. "How about you? I've got a cupcake with your name on it, if there's anything you need."

"What am I gonna wish for? Not to die? Naw, Mabel, I am as pleased as a man can be. Lived a good life. My girls is all taken care of, and my wife's waiting for me on the other side. Save your cupcake. Give it to this one, maybe." He pointed to me. "Wishes are best spent on the young."

"What's that?" I asked, wondering how I got included in their conversation about relatives and cupcakes.

Mabel fidgeted like a woman squished between a rock and a hard place. Then, suddenly, she seemed to decide something.

"Belle," Mabel began. "This may seem like an odd question. But—if I could give you a cupcake that would grant you a wish, what would you do with it?"

"I never had much use for wishes." With a laugh, I joked, "Why? You got any cupcakes like that?"

"Yes." She *wasn't* laughing. In fact, she seemed to be waiting on an answer, for real.

Before I'd met my pain imps, the notion would have been downright crazy. But now? A wish cake seemed only mildly peculiar with a slight chance of possible.

I squinted at her. "You really have some kind of wishing cakes?"

Mabel nodded. "It's a sort of . . . Sass town magic."

"Huh."

"I've been thinking about offering you one, Belle, but—"

She seemed to be apologizing. It took me a second to figure out what for.

"I understand," I said. "You're saving it for someone specialer." A friend who was more than a charity guest, probably.

"No! It's not that, at all! It's only—sometimes it's better to *heal* things, rather than simply fixing them." She bit her lip. "Do you understand what I mean?"

I gave it a think. "It might be like . . . if you gave a dog medicine for his sick stomach. He'll just get sick again if he

90

keeps eating filth. You got to remedy his stupid, if you want him to *stay* fixed."

Mabel agreed that was a very creative example.

"Surely is," said Crispy. "I used to have a dog like that. He just wouldn't learn."

At that moment, a lady with a pink VOLUNTEER T-shirt appeared in the doorway. She greeted Crispy by name and said she was checking to see if he needed anything. I could tell from her expression that she was ready to move a mountain if it would give the man even a sliver of comfort or relief.

Folks here seem to really care about these sick people, I thought. I'd never even known there were such places as this.

Come to think of it, almost every day now, I was bumping into *something* I'd never known before. Seeds sprouting under my care. People giving without expecting something in return. It was like swapping howdies with the world for the very first time.

"You go ahead and keep your magic cakes, Mabel," I decided. "I've got enough to chew on."

"Well." She looked at me with something like wonder. "All right, then."

Turning to Crispy, I said, "So, uh. I guess there's not much, at your age, that you ain't done before, Crispy. Must make this dying thing fairly interesting, huh?"

Mabel's jaw dropped.

But Crispy only gave an elder's wise nod and said, "Hadn't thought of it like that. I reckon you're right."

"Are you scared?" I wanted to know.

"Scared? Of dying?" Crispy repeated. "I used to be, when I was a younger man. But now? Naw. I'm ready to see what's next. Ready to see my wife again. And my mama. So many good people waiting for me there."

I considered the chances that a certain someone might be waiting there for me. Maybe he'd be smiling. Maybe I could even give him his jacket back.

"So, you're fairly sure you won't just wink out?" I asked. That was Nina's notion of dying. *Seventy-some years of bullpuck and misery—then Nothing!* she'd snarled more than once.

"Wink out. Hmm," Crispy mused.

I happened to glance at Mabel just then. She was leaning forward in her seat, biting her knuckle. Her expression was a puzzlement. Part amusement, part alarm, I thought it might have been.

"No," Crispy went on. "Winking out's for things like lightbulbs and car batteries. Folks are more than that. We've got a spark of Greatness nobody can turn out." He smoothed his covers. "Yes, I'm sure of that."

I brooded on that, some. I might have a spark, I decided, but it probably wasn't too great.

"But I bet you were a good man your whole life. Me, I've done some things wrong," I told him. "Winking out might be better! What if I ended up someplace bad?"

Crispy cast his rheumy eyes my way. "I wasn't always so good. But the older I get, and the closer I come to the end,

92

the more I hear a certain truth, over and over again, sung like a choir through the boughs of time."

"What's that, sir?"

A hush had fallen over the room—maybe even over the whole hospice. Where I'd half heard TV chatter and beeping machines before, now there seemed to be nothing but a breath held and listening.

Crispy held up a gnarled hand. "Only love is real."

Mabel exhaled softly.

"But the other thing, Belle, the other thing?" the old man went on. "Those bad things you've done, you don't have to let them stand. A lot of times you can go back and make things right. And where you can't, at least you can do different next time. If you get the chance."

What would that mean, if I went back and made things right? Should I confess to the people I stole from? Or tell Sheriff Thrasher I deserved juvie, after all?

I was cogitating on that when I noticed that a deep red pain imp had flared up just over Crispy's heart. He shut his eyes and shook his head a little.

Something moved in me, right then, maybe a different sort of loco. It wouldn't let me just sit in my chair while that dying man suffered.

"Crispy . . ." I slipped from my seat and knelt down beside his chair. "I can see you got a pain on your heart." I didn't dare pluck it off with Mabel watching.

He nodded, his eyes still closed. "One thing I could have

made right. *Should* have made right. Won't never have the chance now."

"What is it?" I asked. "Could I help?"

"No," Crispy sighed. Then, all at once, he perked up and his imp paled. "Well—maybe. Maybe you could! Mabel, would you go to the closet and fetch the leather book on the top shelf?"

Mabel was up in a flash.

"Young lady, if I tell you what to say, will you write something down and take it somewhere for me?"

It took Crispy some time to collect his thoughts and give us his words. Then it took me some time to get it neat enough—and spelled right—so he could sign it. But finally we had it done. He cried when he read it.

"Yes. Thank you, both of you. Yes."

"Is there anything else we can do for you?" Mabel asked Crispy.

"I might take one of your dee-licious peanut butter cookies if you brung any with you," he answered.

"There's a whole box of them down in the kitchen. I'll go grab you some. You want to come, Belle?"

I was fixin' to reply when Crispy said, "Let her keep me company."

"Glad to," I said.

After Mabel left, Crispy said to me, "The address is in that leather book, all right?"

"Yessir. I already looked at it. I even know the place," I told him.

"Good, good." He settled back into his chair, a bundle of little old man and crocheted yarn. "Now, then. While our Mabel's gone, perhaps you'll tell me how you knew I had a pain on my heart."

"I—" I considered saying it was a guess, but it struck me that lying to a dying man might be on life's list of *Things Not to Do*. "I saw it."

His eyes squinched ever so slightly. "You did?"

"Um-hmm. I can still see it. In fact, now that Mabel is gone, I was thinking I might take it off of you." I half smiled nervously. "If you'll let me."

"You can do that?"

I nodded.

"You *are* a friend of Magical Mabel's, ain't ya?"

I didn't know what to say to that. "So, can I pluck it off?"

"Would you please?" He seemed to try to hold his chest up for me, but the effort didn't amount to much.

It didn't matter. The imp was plain as day. Though it was real pale, now that Crispy's letter was finished. I reached out and gave the imp a yank. It came off nice and easy.

"Ahh—" Crispy sighed contentedly.

He was smiling asleep when Mabel came back.

As we made our way out, I noticed that the door to the near-dead skeleton-person's room was still open. The pain imp rippled like mad on their belly, redder than before.

"Hold up a second?" I asked Mabel.

"Sure," she said, looking curious, but asking nothing.

I tiptoed into the room. A peculiar, sweet smell hung in the air.

"Hey," I whispered to the old soul on the bed. "I just wanna help you with something." Real quick-like, I snatched up the imp and shoved it into my pocket.

Nothing changed, except maybe the slightest softening of their breath. But I couldn't help believing that, inside them—or wherever they were—they felt a little better.

"Okay," I told Mabel as I left the room.

"Everything all right?"

I thought it over. *Was* everything all right? *Could* it be all right? This hospice was full of dying people, after all. I could hear a lady crying even now. But in another way, inside of me, just for now, everything *was* all right.

"Yup," I replied.

On a whim, I reached out and took Mabel's hand into both of my own.

"Thanks for bringing me here."

At 2:17 that morning, I awoke, my loco bearing down on me so hard I thought I might die of it. Right away, it started talking to me in pictures, remembering things I didn't even know I knew: Mabel's crystal earbobs were sitting on the edge of the bathroom sink. A fifty-dollar gift certificate for Dress Up was tucked into a notebook in the kitchen junk drawer. Two strings of beads hung from the rearview mirror of the pickup truck outside.

I didn't even have to shake off my sleep. My loco was wide awake. I jumped out of bed and tiptoed toward the bathroom. Right away, the pain in my head let off so I could think clear enough to sneak.

The earbobs were right where my loco said they'd be. Hoo, they were pretty, twinkling in the glow of the nightlight. They'd look real pretty in my stash, too.

Like a thing with its own mind, my hand reached out to take them—

—And stopped.

I had made a promise. A promise to try. I said I would talk to someone before I stole.

My head pounded with the demand of my loco. The first bits of crazy flickered at the sides of my vision.

I happened to see myself in the mirror. Pain imps clung to my forehead, to spots above my ears, at the base of my skull in the back. And there was one, a real big one, a-rippling over my heart. Without a thought, I reached for that one first and gave it a tug. Or, rather, I tried to.

I couldn't grasp it.

I tried the others in turn. Ears. Forehead. Skull. My hand passed right through them. A little frantic, I turned away from the mirror and I looked down at my chest.

There wasn't a single imp upon me.

Then I looked back in the mirror—and there they all were again.

Meanwhile, the loco was just a-flying down its track, fixin' to squash me. The imps would have to wait.

I ran to Mabel's closed door and lifted my hand to knock—but couldn't. Was I *really* gonna wake a pregnant lady at two in the a.m.?

Yes, yes, I have to! part of me insisted.

But I just couldn't set my knuckles to the door.

What about somebody else? I could call Jimmy! (What, and wake all four Orrs in the wee hours? How would I explain *that* to Desiree?) Or maybe JoBeth would be working dispatch! The police were open round the clock, right? (And what if it's not JoBeth? *Hello, dispatcher, I'm fixin' to commit a crime?*)

Ugh! I stormed into the living room.

Ugh! Then back into the bathroom.

I snatched up Mabel's earbobs and held them tight in my fist. Oh, I wanted *so* bad to start me a new stash! I knew just where I'd put it, too. In the back of the potting shed outside, there was a old tackle box, covered in cobwebs. I could clear out the underneath section real easy, but leave the stuff in the top cubbies to hide my borrows. Mabel would never even know.

She said her great-grandma gave her those earrings, the Voice reminded me.

Ugh! I threw down the earrings and quiet-stomped into my room.

Atop the dresser, seven pain imps rippled in the mayo jar.

"Listen, you!" I poked my face at the jar. "I ain't got no one to talk to but you, so you it's gonna be!"

They didn't reply, but that didn't surprise me none.

"My loco is screaming!" I told them. "My head hurts! The whole world's asleep and those earbobs are calling my name! I don't understand it! Things was going so good! I was feeling fine!"

I gripped the jar so hard my knuckles turned white. "I don't want to go back to 'Bagoville! I want to stay here where things are lit up and soft. I hate that dark, stank RV! I hate what Nina done and what she said! I hate that she's my mother! I hate my whole life, every blame second of it until I met Desiree in that stupid, yellow laundrymat!"

I was gasping for air now.

"I know I only knowed Desiree for a short time, but she's my crazy friend! I never had a crazy friend!"

My eyes teared up. I could barely make out the imps.

Whisper-shouting at the sky, I cried, "Please don't take my friend! Please don't take my new life! Please don't make me steal! *Please!*"

Tears streaming, I set down the jar. It *thunk*ed with a louder noise than I'd expected, and I jumped. *Dingnation!* Did I just wake Mabel, after I'd tried so hard not to? And now that I thought on it, how loud *had* I been talking? I wasn't even sure.

I sat still and quiet for a time, listening, hoping not to hear the sounds of a pregnant lady's sleep disturbed. Thankfully, none came.

I stretched and wiped my tears, taking in the room afresh. Starlight filtering in from the blinds. The ticking sound of Travis's old-style clock. Desiree's rainbow rock. Jimmy's book.

On a whim, I reached for it. Some words were embossed in the cover. I turned on a light so I could read them. *The Big Book*, they said. And in smaller print, *Twelve Steps Anonymous*.

Why not? I figured. *I ain't getting to sleep anytime soon.* I opened the book.

We discovered we were powerless over our addictions. Our best efforts to stop them had failed. We needed help from a bigger, Higher Power.

Truth to tell, it both made sense and it didn't. I figured *Higher Power* was something like the knowing Voice Mabel and I both heard, and Crispy's *love*, the only thing that was real. But how did you get a thing like that to help you? It seemed to me the Voice came when it wanted and slipped

100

off just as quick. And as for love, that was a thing whose acquaintance I'd barely ever made.

And! *And!* Even if you *did* know how to get the help of this Bigger Power, how were you supposed to wait for its pleasure when twenty tons of loco was bearing down on you?

I surely did not know.

But I read some more of that book anyway, until I fell asleep. And when I woke up, the loco was mostly quiet.

MISSION

"Belle! Come look!" Mabel called from the front porch.

Barefooted and bedheaded, I stepped outside. Mabel was holding one of my potted weeds up to the sunlight.

"Looky here!" she said. "Your plants are thriving!"

It was true! The flowers had looked so forlorn before, plucked as they had been from the ground. But today they were upright and strong, their pink-petaled faces turned gladly toward the sky.

A notion took me. "Hey, uh, Mabel?"

"Mmm?"

"What if I took one to Crispy's friend? And one to Desiree? Would you mind parting with them nice pots?"

"Pssh," Mabel huffed. "I've got more flowerpots than you can shake a stick at. Take 'em!" She set the flower back down on the porch. "Are you planning on running Crispy's errand today? I'd be happy to give you a lift."

Right quick, I brain-navigated a way to get there without

passing by the shopping district. "No, I think I've got it, thanks."

She took off her hat and wiped her brow. "Do you have time for breakfast first?"

Putting on a surly expression, I crossed my arms. "Mabel, do you know what I had for breakfast the day we met?"

"No."

"Two handfuls of Monkey Puffs and a few swigs of co-cola."

"Oh?" I could see she was doing her dangedest to hide a pained expression.

"I reckon I would have to be a mighty right fool to miss out on one of your fine meals." I grinned.

She laughed.

"So, what is it this morning?" I asked. "Fancy eggs or fancy muffins?"

I told Mabel I'd be back to work after my visits with Crispy's friend and Desiree. She kindly packed a double lunch for me and Desiree to share.

"After all that flattery, how could I deprive you of a homemade lunch?" she wanted to know.

With Crispy's letter in my pocket and an address in my head—not to mention a bag of food hung over my elbow and one flowering, potted weed under each arm—I departed on foot.

The lady's house was only one block off Main, so it was easy to find, but a mite tempting to my loco.

Oh, Bigger Power, I said. *Keep my feet on this here road.*

Fortunately, there were a few things to distract me. The weather was fair, but there were some grayish, flat-looking clouds in the distance. I looked at them real hard so I could describe them to Desiree and ask if they meant rain. I thought she'd like that.

Next, I saw a turtle slow-tailing it across the road. Even in a Podunk like Sass, a pace like that could get him squashed. No sooner had I scooped him up and deposited him beside a water-filled ditch than I spotted a man in his yard, watering a familiar-looking shrub within an inch of its life.

I had to work up the nerve, but I finally did walk over to him and say, "Sir, I work at a plant nursery, and my boss told me that plant can't tolerate much water."

"That so?" he said, looking at the hose as if it done him wrong.

I knelt down and felt the ground. "I'd be surprised if it lives out the week. Good news, though: you do seem to have a green thumb for the roses." Nodding in the direction of some lively blooms, I suggested, "Ought to plant more of them. Once it dries out, this spot here might not be bad."

"Why, I thank you kindly!" He seemed to mean it, too.

I was reflecting on how far-fetched it seemed that Hush Cantrell could offer advice about anything except sneak thieving, when suddenly on my right side, there appeared the house I was looking for.

It was a large place, bigger than Mabel's and the Orrs' combined. Porches wrapped around not just the first floor but the second story, too. An old, faded sign hung just outside the fence, reading THE REST EASY BOARDINGHOUSE.

I went up to the door and knocked with the toe of my shoe.

Through an open window, I heard somebody shuffling up long before they appeared. Finally the door did open, and a pink-haired lady with a cane stood before me. Pain imps fluttered on both of her hips. She gave me a thorough going-over, pausing for quite some time to mull on my weeds.

"Yes?" she asked, a little suspicious.

"Missus Roxie Fuller?" I inquired.

"Yes."

Juggling my armfuls of stuff, I pulled the paper from my pocket. "I have a letter here for you. From Mister Crispy Freye. Can I give it to you?"

"Crispy Freye, you say?" She squinted into her memory. "You mean *Dalton* Freye?" All at once, a deep red pain imp flared over her heart.

"I don't rightly know, ma'am. Probably, if you know the name. Can I give you the letter?" I repeated.

"All . . . right." She cane-walked onto the porch. "My glasses are lost, though. Could you read it to me?"

I told her I could, and followed her down to a few wicker chairs on the shady side of the house.

"You know Dalton?" she asked as she sat.

"Not very well, but yes, I know him."

"And he asked you to bring me a letter? Me, Roxanne Fuller?"

"Uh-huh."

"Curious. I haven't spoken to him since—" She shook her head. "Neverhoo. What's he got to say?"

I set down the plants and unfolded the letter, sparing half a glance for that pain imp over her heart. How sudden it sprung up!

"Dear Roxie," I read. "Many years ago, when we were kids, your sister came to me and told me you thought I was handsome, and that you planned to marry me someday. All my friends was there and they started a-laughing. I was mighty embarrassed, and knew for sure they'd rib me worse unless I came up with something clever—or cruel—to say. So I did.

"I said, 'Roxie Fuller is fat and ugly. Besides, I'd never marry a boardinghouse girl!'

"That got me off the hook with my friends, but what I didn't know, until a minute later, was that you were there, hiding behind a tree and listening to the whole thing. I saw you cry, Roxie, and I saw you run away. And because of it, I know how bad I hurt your feelings.

"You never did talk to me again after that, and you were in your rights not to. But because you kept away, and because I was so ashamed, I never got to apologize, or to tell you the truth. So, here it is.

"I was a coward. A despisable coward and a foot licker, desperate not to be made fun of. And you, Roxie, you were neither ugly nor fat. You were the prettiest girl in our year, with the sweetest dimples I ever did see. But even more important than that, you were always so brave, so easeful with different kinds of folks. The truth is, I _admired_—"

"That's underlined," I explained.

"I _admired_ that you were a boardinghouse girl. How many curious and interesting people you must have met! Not at all like my humdrum upbringing! I admired you so much, Roxie. It tore me up when you stopped speaking to me, because I liked you so very much.

"Someday, when we meet on the other side, I hope to apologize to you in person, and you'll see how sincere I am. Until then, this letter will have to do. You were always beautiful, Roxie, in every way that a young girl can be. I am so sorry if I made you believe any different.

"With every sincere wish for your happiness,

"Crispy"

When I looked up, Roxie had one hand on her heart and the other curved above her eyes. The pain imp flickered pale-dark, pale-dark.

"Read it again," she whispered. "Please."

I did. By the time I finished, the pain imp over her heart had vanished. Not merely pale, but clean gone.

"Don't that beat all!" I said.

"It sure does," Roxie replied. There was a kind of awe in her voice as she added, "I forgot all about that."

I canted my head. "Part of you didn't."

She made a sound that might have been a laugh or a sob. "You're right! Seventy years later, part of me still remembered." After a time, she ran her hands down her face. "Well, thank you, young lady. *Thank you.* Now, tell me, how is Dalton and what's he up to? Why did he send you?"

"Oh, well, ma'am," I said. "Crispy's up at the Pitney hospice, fixin' to die. I reckon he's doing well in spite of it—"

"Hospice? Dying!" She set her hand on her heart, where a new pain imp appeared. "Can I see him? Is he taking visitors?"

"I think so. Me and Mabel Holt sat with him just yesterday."

She gripped her cane and gave it a shake. "Well, it's good, then. It's good that you came. Thank you, uh, what's your name?"

"Hush Cantrell."

"Thank you, Hush. I'd offer you a blueberry muffin, but once a body's got a bed in Pitney, there's no time to lose!" She pushed herself to standing and headed for her house.

My flowers wobbled in the draft that the slamming door left behind.

"Hey! One of these is for you!" I called out, holding up one of the plants.

I heard her make some reply, but precisely what she said, I never found out.

Her big Cadillac peeled out from her garage before I was halfway down the block.

Me and Desiree had a picnic lunch in the Orrs' front yard, sitting on a sheet Becky brought out for us. Desiree made the potted flower our centerpiece—it pleased her so mightily, she'd refused to leave it inside while we ate.

I asked her about the grayish clouds—the rain was headed away from us, not toward, she said—and she told me about her first day soothing equines for *Horse Dentist*.

"There was this one mare, named Pepper Shakes," she said. "So beautiful, except her teeth were yellow and she had a big cavity. At first I couldn't calm her down, but then I remembered how, when my daddy first took me to the dentist and I was so scared, he sang a certain song and it helped me feel better. So I sang that song to the horse, *real* soft, and she went all still and mild, and the dentist did his work just fine. Sometimes there's magic in the homeliest things, you know?"

In fact, I was fairly sure I did not know, but I was growing accustomed to Desiree's peculiar, glad way of looking at things.

"So! What about the pain imps?" she asked.

"What about them?"

"I keep feeling like we should *do* something, now that we know they're there."

I nodded. Since the hospice, I'd been feeling that way, too. I told Desiree about Crispy and the skeleton person. I also mentioned how Roxie Fuller's pain imps came and went that morning.

"Have you thought about just telling people you can see them?" Desiree asked me.

"No way, nohow! Sass folk already think plenty of things about me. I don't want to add *crazy* to the list."

"I wish we had some way to *prove* they were there. It might help you feel more confident," she said. "What we need is a good scientific study. Samples and measurements and peer-reviewed journals."

I laughed. "You're spending too much time with that dentist. It ain't science we need, it's—"

"What?" Desiree tugged at my sleeve.

"I don't know." It took some time to find my tongue. "I think we need . . . a scam."

She looked at me sideways.

I went on, "We need to get those imps off of people, get folks feeling better. It's like you said the other day, about putting a stop to pain. But it's like I said, too. We can't just go, 'Excuse me, there's an invisible thing dangling off of you, Missus Smith. Let me just get a little personal here and pluck it off your boob.'"

Desiree giggled. And then I giggled. And then—oh, Lordy—we got caught in one of those laugh traps, where you can't stop no matter how hard you try. And Becky came outside and asked what was so funny, and we laughed even harder, our eyes a-watering, and us not able to squeak out the words *We can't stop!* To this day, I can't tell you exactly what got hold of us, but all that laughing, I do believe it was like vitamins for our souls.

"But you were just joshing about a scam, right?" Desiree asked, once we'd caught our breath.

"Nuh-uh," I said. "We need a good way of tricking people into letting me get close enough to pull off the imps without jangling their warning bells. Like, if we were measuring them for clothes, that would do it."

"We could . . . offer a free measurement service."

"But what for? We got no clothes to sell."

"Oh, right." All of a sudden, her eyes got wide. "Okay! How about this? A hugging booth! They had one at the Valentine's festival last year."

"Hmm," I said, trying not to hurt Desiree's feelings

by spurning the idea too fast. But did we *truly* want to go around hugging drunks and cat ladies? Because you *know* that's who'd be coming. "I think some people's sensitive about hugging."

Desiree seemed a mite disappointed, but she let it pass. "What, then?"

I gave it a long think. "Too bad we don't have no cause to pat them down, like the police do."

We were munching Mabel's fancy cookies when a certain sight flashed before my eyes: JoBeth Haines, on the day I got busted, stuffing my borrow list between the pages of a yoga magazine.

"I know! We'll teach them yoga! It's real popular!" I exclaimed. "While we're helping folks get into the positions and whatnot, I can pull off the imps!"

"You know yoga?" Desiree asked, looking somewhat awed.

"Well, no." That did gum up the works.

"Hey!" Desiree got so excited right then, she squeezed her cookie to crumbs. "Ma has a yoga video! I bet she'll let us borrow it. She never uses it!"

"Okay, what's this called?" Desiree bent over, hands and feet on the floor, butt pointed at the sky.

We'd watched Becky's yoga video twice and tried out all the poses, so now we were quizzing each other. We had to look like professionals, after all.

"Dog something. Dog . . . downward-facing dog!"

"And this one?" She lifted one leg and moved it in a circle.

I thought it over. "That ain't no pose."

"Right!" she said. "Hush, I think we're ready!"

I reckoned we were, too. "Now all we need is a place to hold the class."

Desiree tapped her lips with a fingertip. "I guess I could ask my ma if we could use the yard."

"Naw. You let me worry about that." I thought I might have a notion. "Meantime, though, could you think up some advertising to get folks interested in the class?"

"Advertising? Oh, definitely." She gave me a business-like nod. "Before I wanted to be a horse witch, I was very nearly an adman!"

That afternoon, me and Mabel were stuffing herbs into jars and pouring oil over them.

"Smells good enough to eat," I told her.

"That's the idea." She gave one of her jars a sniff. "Mmm! Ever since I got pregnant, I just cannot get enough of the smell of olive oil."

"Maybe your baby's gonna be Italian."

She looked up to see if I was joking. I grinned. She shook her head and went back to her oil smelling.

She was unscrewing and re-screwing a jar lid when

she asked, "So, how are you doing, Belle? With your loco and such?"

I grabbed a handful of basil. "Last night was a bad time, but today I feel real good."

"Last night?" She looked worried. "Did you go out?"

I shook my head. "Naw. Nothing like that. It was—" I chewed on the inside of my cheek. "You won't get mad, right?"

"There's no penalty for honesty in this house," Mabel promised.

"It was your earbobs. The crystal ones you had sitting on the sink."

She was quiet for a time. "I believe they're still in there."

I nodded. "They are. No thanks to my loco."

A truck rumbled down the street that ran past Mabel's place. Through the fence gaps, I could just make out the outlines of the rattling cattle hauler it towed behind it. *Must be a noisy way for a critter to travel*, I thought.

"So, what'd you do?" she asked.

"What? Oh. I did the dangedest thing. I talked to—" But, for some reason, I still wasn't ready to tell Mabel about the imps. Honesty didn't mean you had to tell everyone every little thing, did it? A body was entitled to some personal matters, weren't they? "That jar you gave me."

"How creative," she said, and she wasn't even poking fun.

"And, uh, also I read some of this book Jimmy Orr gave me. It's called *The Big Book*. You ever read that?"

She nodded. "What'd you think of it?"

I recalled one of the book's passages. "It was simple—but not easy."

She gave a little chuckle. "Ain't that the truth."

Another truck drove by with another noisy livestock hauler. *Poor cows are gonna go deaf.*

"So, uh," I said, "I was wondering if I might ask you a favor."

"Ask away," Mabel said.

"You know that carport you have back there? The one next to the shed?"

"Um-hmm."

"How would you feel if I cleaned that off, maybe set your plug-in fan out there, and held me a yoga class? It would only be once a week, and I could ask folks to park around back—"

"I'm sorry." Mabel held up a hand. "I just need to rewind for a sec. Did you say *yoga* class?"

"Yoga. Yes," I told her. "Me and Desiree were watching a video of it and we got to thinking we might be able to teach folks. Help them have less pain and whatnot." I couldn't have been more honest. I was only withholding certain bits I wasn't ready to share. Wasn't the seeing of invisible pain imps a personal matter, after all?

"I . . . don't know what to say to that," Mabel remarked.

I felt a touch disappointed. "Guess I could use the Town Hall."

"No, you can use the carport. Of course you can," she said. "But you'll stick to the easy stuff, won't you? I mean, you're not really qualified. Yoga instructors usually work at it for a few years, at least, before they start teaching."

"I reckon we're more qualified than most in town," I said truthfully. "You may not have noticed, but a lot of people in Sass are old. Or fat. Probably most of them wouldn't know a downward-facing dog if they sat on it."

She smiled. "Well, you have a point there." Snipping a sprig of rosemary, she said, "So you'd sweep out the carport?"

"Yes, ma'am. Real clean."

"And you really would be careful? You wouldn't put Roxie Fuller in a headstand, for instance?"

I laughed. "No, ma'am. Super careful."

"Could I come to the class?"

"Sure!"

She sighed real deep, but it had a certain good humor to it. "All right, Belle Cantrell. You've got your space. Let's start us a yoga class."

YOGI

It was a good thing both me and Desiree were there to teach yoga because those folks needed a *lot* of help, and I don't just mean me plucking off their pain imps.

"All right, that's real good, Ham," I said as encouraging as I could. "But if you want to call it warrior pose, you got to bend at the knee." I flexed to show him how. "I think you ought not hold your breath so. You're getting real red in the face."

Ham Quimby, a big man with spiky hair, still didn't manage to bend his knee—but he did lean so far forward that he nearly squashed poor Mabel when he fell. Gamely rising again, he muttered to himself, "Rome wasn't built in a day!"

Even so, things were going fine. Not only did the carport clean up real good, but Mabel had helped me set up three plug-in fans, mounted high up on a beam, so folks could stay nice and cool. She'd also loaned me her radio and a bunch of plinky-plunk music. People seemed to like that.

Desiree made the rounds, fixing poses where pain wasn't

the problem, but only sorry listening skills or lack of coordination. Me, I showed off the positions up front and did most of the talking, strolling around now and then to snatch off a pain imp.

"Imagine you's a tree now, real strong and straight," I said, wobbling on one foot with my hands pressed together. "This here's called tree position."

I caught a glimpse of a pain imp on one lady's neck. Miz Buchanan, I thought Desiree had called her.

"Miz B," I said, walking up from behind. "You look like a turtle in his shell. You got to stick your neck *out*." I swiped my hand under her hair, tapped her neck, and scooped up the imp.

She turned her head real sudden. "What'd you do there? Hey! What'd you do?"

Everyone stopped to look, especially Mabel, who had already winced more than once as folks wobbled and creaked.

"I, uh, I fixed your prana," I said, thinking faster than I knew I could. "How's that feel now?"

She rolled her head around. "It's the best I've felt in an age!" Now she rolled it the other way. "Fixed my prana, huh?"

Mabel raised an eyebrow.

"Hey! Hush!" a man called. "Come fix my prana, too."

"Me too, Hush!"

"My leg prana's troubling me. Can you fix that?"

I made my way up to the front and quietly dropped Miz B's imp into the mayo jar, which I'd left there earlier.

118

On my way to check a lady's "prana," I traded smiles with Desiree. She gave me a thumbs-up.

At the end of class, I told everyone to lay on their backs on their mats. "It's called corpse pose, but that's what you call a symbolic name, and not an instruction. Everyone walks out of here on two feet, y'all understand?" One very old lady was looking far too comfortable for my peace of mind.

Everyone chuckled.

I turned up the music. "Let yourself be floppy. And heavy, like you weigh a million pounds. Now, we're gonna stay like this for a time, so just close your eyes and reeee-lax."

From where I stood, I gave everyone a last good looking-over. I couldn't see a single pain imp left in the bunch, and my jar was a darn sight fuller than it had been. A number of our eight students had grins upon their faces, and every one was looking so content I wanted to whoop. Of course I didn't. That would have ruined the effect.

As the yogis collected their towels and whatnot, more than one of them drifted over to the mayo jar, screwed it open—*Lordy, no! The imps'll get out!*—and dropped a few dollars in before sealing it up again. I was relieved to see the pain imps weren't of a mind to escape—not a single one broke free.

Desiree and me were working out a way to split up the money—some for her, some for me, some for Mabel since it was her carport—when Mabel herself walked up.

"Belle?"

"Ma'am?" I tried to grin, but something told me this might not be good.

"We need to talk."

After Desiree scooted home, Mabel set out the fixin's for tea, then sat across from me at the dining table. Her face was as serious as I'd ever seen it, and I couldn't think of nothin' else, except I was busted.

"I need you to be honest with me," she said.

"Very honest," I promised.

"There's something you haven't told me, isn't there?"

All at once, I exploded into a panic. "But, Mabel, it don't have *nothin'* to do with my loco and I felt sure I was allowed to have *some* things that was my own private thoughts and I swear, I *swear,* no harm's come to anyone, nor could come—"

"Belle—"

"But if you really feel I've been a fabler, I'll get down on my knees right now and ask for your forgiveness—" I started sliding from my seat.

"Belle!"

"Yeah?"

She gave a saddish half smile. "I know a healer when I see one."

I jerked my chin back. *Me? A healer?*

"I am a little sorry you didn't feel comfortable confiding in me, but we haven't known each other that long. And yes, you're right. Everyone's allowed to keep some thoughts private." She paused. "Honey, relax. I'm not going to take anything from you."

I realized I was holding myself ramrod-straight. I tried to settle back in my chair. "All right."

She blinked a few times. "Um. So, I guess what I want to say is: A healer has an important job. It's no small thing, caring for others." Mabel shrugged and shook her head all at once. "Lord knows you're savvy, Belle, but you're young, too. And I'm enough of a healer myself—with herbs, not like what you do with your hands—to know you shouldn't tackle this all on your own."

"I'm fairly used to tackling things on my own," I told her.

"I know. And I respect that," she said sincerely. "But some things we aren't meant to do by our lonesome. Like your loco. You needed some help with that, right?"

"Ye-ah, but . . ." I was struggling in my seat again, though I can't say why, precisely. It just seemed so important that no one get between me and my imp plucking. As if letting someone meddle with it—especially a grown-up someone— might crush the bloom when it was just beginning to grow.

"Okay, Belle. I see you want to work this out for yourself." She held up a calming hand. "Can we talk about it just a little, though?"

What I really wanted was to go hide under that fine bed she was loaning me, shouting, *Them's my imps!* as I went, but I had a notion that might seem a little nutty. "I guess."

"How long have you had it, this gift?" she asked.

I didn't have to think back very far. "It started the day we met, when we were in the garden and your back twinged you."

"Dear goodness! Not long at all! And you healed me then." She paused. "You did, right?"

I nodded.

"Well . . . you seem to be right on schedule. Sass kids who develop shines—they do tend to find them at twelve or thirteen."

I puzzled over that. "What do you mean, 'shines'?"

"They're, well . . . My mom called them gifts of power," she explained. "But if you look at it simply, it's just a little spark of magic. A thing you can do that, maybe, makes the world a little nicer."

I couldn't help thinking of Desiree's longing to be a horse witch. Was that a shine?

"And your shine is growing plants for healing?" I asked.

"Yes," she answered. "Though I've picked up a bit more magic along the way. My wish cupcakes, for instance." Now Mabel seemed to think for a while. "So, the first time you saw the pain imps, you just knew what to do about them? Intuitively?"

"I don't know that word," I told her.

"It means you understood how to heal people without thinking about it or being told how."

"Oh. Then, yeah. I reckon it was like that. But it's not real complicated, anyway. Just pluck them off."

"And did you do the same thing for that lady in the hospice?" she asked.

"The skeleton person, you mean? Uh-huh. And Crispy, too, when you were out of the room."

She seemed a little surprised by that. "Does it make you tired after you've done it? Do you feel sick at all?"

I thought of the ache in my hand when I held an imp for any time, but that wasn't sick or tired. "No."

"Well, that's good. Some people do, you know." She leaned in. "But you did say you had some bad dreams. How are those?"

I'd had one more dream about Baron Ramey's teeth tearing into raw meat, but that was it. "Mostly all right. Better."

She took a long swig of her tea. "Hmm. I guess everything *seems* okay. Surely your students today were happy enough." She gave a little laugh. "But if you do find yourself in a quandary, or if something just doesn't feel right, send up a flare. Please?"

I told her I would. "But, uh, can I keep teaching yoga?"

She set down her mug with a thump. "Are you kidding? Those people would whup me with their yoga mats if I canceled that class!" She was full-on beaming now. "Did you *see* their faces?"

"Yeah," I said. "That was something, wasn't it?"

INVITED

On one sunny Friday morning, I went into the garden to find Mabel sitting in the crook of her granddaddy apple tree, wedged between two low, chunky branches. She looked right comfortable there among the fruit and leaves.

"Is that safe for a pregnant lady?" I called to her.

"I used a step stool," she called back. "Come join me."

I climbed into the tree and found my spot, a little higher than Mabel, with a sturdy place to rest my setter. It was sort of nice, with the dewy air and whatnot. Apples dangled all around us, glinting red in the morning light.

"I didn't know grown folks climbed trees," I said.

"Wouldn't it be wonderful if more of us did?" Mabel mused. "Maybe you and I should start the Sass Tree Climbers Club. We could meet every Friday and all of us sit in the same tree like a flock of crows."

"Come wintertime, we could tie red and green ribbons in the treetops," I suggested.

She closed her eyes. I thought she might be imagining the trees of Sass decorated for the holidays. "I love that idea."

A soft wind joggled the branches, casting a piece of ripe fruit to the ground.

"One time I stole a Christmas ribbon," I told her. "It was so pretty."

"Did you put it in a tree?"

I shook my head. "Somebody might have found out I stole it. I did keep it inside my coat, though. I liked to look at it."

It was long gone now, of course. In 'Bagoville, even when you had a private stash, nice things had a way of disappearing.

I reached out and plucked an apple. "You make pie from these?"

"One certainly could. I like to use them for cobbler, served warm with plenty of cream."

That woman never seemed to run out of fine ways to fill a belly!

"It's funny, how you used to throw up your food, but you cook so good now," I said.

She leaned her head against a limb. "It took me a long time to make peace with food. I spent a long time doing simple things. Breathing the scents of bread and broth. Cutting open apples to look at the seeds."

With those words, a door of memory opened in my mind.

I said, "My first daddy used to like to plant his apple

125

seeds after he finished eating the apple. I don't think any ever grew, though."

Mabel turned so she could look me in the eye. "Do you ever see him, Belle?"

"Who? My first daddy?"

She nodded.

"Naw. After Nina kicked him out, he went to find work in Colorado. One time I found a paper with his phone number on it, and I called, but the lady who answered said he died from coal sickness."

Mabel sucked a breath through her teeth. "That's a hard way to find out."

"Wasn't no other way I *could* find out." I paused. "I guess."

In the silence, I tapped a few apples and set them bobbling. "Ready for cobbler, I'd say."

She gave a soft smile, but she wasn't ready to change the subject. "Do you miss him?"

I recalled one time I'd missed my first daddy so powerfully, I spent a whole night crying. Nina called me an ugly crybaby and told me to shut up.

"No. I had to stop that," I answered. "I do like to remember certain things about him, though.

"Once, he took me to this ditch out by the highway, and he showed me all the tadpoles swimming there. They were real cute. He said we'd go back later, to see them in their in-betweens. You know, when they're mostly frogs but still with tails? But we never got the chance." All at once, my eyes turned wet. I tried to blink the water away, but that only sent fat tears rolling down my cheeks. "I really wanted to see those frogs with tails!"

"I bet he really wanted to show them to you," Mabel offered.

It was hard to go on having those feelings about lost frogs and my first daddy cast out, then dying. I was almost glad when a pain imp popped up near Mabel's heart. Not for her pain, of course, but because it was something I could remedy.

"I'm sorry, Mabel. I think my story hurt you some. I'll be glad to take that away." I reached for her imp.

Before I could grasp it, she caught my hand in both of her hands. "Belle. Wait."

"But—"

She gave my fingers a squeeze. "If it's all right with you, I'd like to keep this pain. To be sad, together with you. Is that all right?"

It didn't make any sense, and I told her so. "Pain is terrible, Mabel. Why would you ever want to keep it?"

She thought for a time. "You remember how we were talking about weeds? How we might not want them in the garden, but they still have their place?" When I nodded, she said, "I think pain has its place, too. Sometimes it needs to stay awhile. When we stop it before its time, we become less able to feel other important things. Even good things, like joy."

I shook my head. Pain never gave *me* no joy. "I don't know about that."

"That's okay. Friends don't have to agree on everything." She let go my hand. "But I still want to keep my sad for a while."

So, I sat with her there, among the apples, and let her have her pain. Even if I didn't want my own grief, I surely couldn't leave a friend alone while she wrestled with her sorrow.

· · ·

Later that day, while Mabel and I were picking apples for cobbler, the phone rang. Mabel went in to answer it, but then she reappeared just as quickly.

She handed me the phone. "Call for you."

"Hello?" I answered.

"Guess what!" the caller said first thing.

"Desiree?" I asked, distracted by the sad, flopping leaves of a nearby plant that had looked fine only yesterday.

"Yes, it's Desiree," she laughed. "Guess what!"

I set the plant aside for Mabel to look at later. "I guess . . . you got something you want to tell me."

I could almost hear her rolling her eyes—in a kindly way, of course. "You're not very good at this game. Really, now. Guess."

"Okay, wait." I thought for a second. "I got it. One of your horses did something funny on the dentist show."

"Well, yeah. Rooney did try to eat my hair," she admitted. "But that's not what I was going to say. Guess!"

"Desiree," I said, fairly sure I would only go on disappointing her, "I got a sick plant to care for, so maybe you could just tell me."

"Oh. A sick plant? *Oh*." She sounded truly sorrowful.

"It'll be all right. Tell me what you're so excited about."

"Well, I don't know if you can come now, with your sick plant and all," she began. "But tonight's the start of the fair, and we go every year, and my ma said maybe you should go with us, and then you could spend the night!"

"I—" I couldn't find any words. There was so much packed in there. Go to the fair? Do it as part of a family? Spend the night at a friend's house? Those things just didn't happen to a girl like me.

I tried to imagine myself getting on one of those fair rides. Or eating those foods that smelled so good when I sniffed them on the breeze. I saw people winning prizes and eating cotton candies—and tried to picture myself as one of them. Just as fast as I conjured it, the image got wiped away.

Ain't nothing there for 'Bagoville girls. Nor for sneak thieves. Hush Cantrell doesn't go to fairs or throw a ball for a prize. That's for people who have got. And the only reason I got anything is because it's on loan from Mabel.

"I can't go. Sorry," I said flatly.

"Because of your plant."

"Yeah, that's right." Even though it wasn't right, at all. I'd just told my friend a flat-out lie. Even more proof that I wasn't fit for a fair.

"Oh, Hush. Are you sure Mabel couldn't watch the plant for just a little while? The fair only comes one time a year."

"Sorry," I answered. "It's a responsibility, you know?" And there I was, *still* lying to her. Of course Mabel could care for the plant. She had tended her plants before I came along and she surely could again.

Desiree sighed. "I understand. I'll let you get back to your work. Bye."

I felt like the sorriest liar who ever saved themselves from having a heap of fun.

I walked over and gave the phone back to Mabel.

"Got something for you to look at," I said.

Mabel studied the floppy plant and diagnosed it as having outgrown its pot. It took all of fifteen minutes to transplant it.

"It'll be better than new in a couple days," Mabel promised me.

"It don't need nothing else?" I asked, hoping to turn my lie to a truth.

"No," she answered. "At this point, too much attention would be as bad as too little. We'll give it a good watering tomorrow, but that's all."

I nodded, looking down at my shoes.

"Did something happen, Belle?" Mabel wanted to know.

I thought about denying it, but I'd had enough of fabling for the time being. "Yeah. I had . . ." I rummaged through my thoughts. "Can you tell me something?"

She nodded, dusting potting soil off her hands.

"All right. So, imagine a person is hungry and poor," I told her. "And they get invited to a big buffet, with all kinds of good food. But only for one night. And they know they could have their fill for that one night, and it would be real fine. But then, the next day, they'll go back to being poor and hungry, with only the memory of that good food—and the knowing that other people were still eating good, but not her. What would you say to that?"

"I'd say that's a tough place to be," Mabel replied.

"Right! And so maybe when someone invites you to this buffet, it's easier just to say you can't go, that you have stuff to do, even if that's not one hundred percent true. That's probably what you'd do, right?" I asked hopefully.

"Hmm." Mabel blinked a few times as she gave it some thought. "I don't know for sure. I mean, it is a thing people do, trying to avoid pain by holding back from living. But . . ." She tilted sideways one way, then the other, as if she was weighing something.

"But what?"

"I don't think we can be sure that *a* buffet is the *only* buffet, ever. Surprises come along all the time. I didn't know you'd be staying here with me, but here we are. That's a good thing I'd never expected."

"Yeah," I sort of agreed. "But some people have more good surprises than others. Some people, it's just one long life of sorrow."

"Not *all* sorrow," she countered. "Even *one* buffet means it's not all sorrow."

I jerked my chin back. "Well—"

"What if by going to the buffet, you—she—meets someone who invites her to another buffet?" Mabel asked. "Or she learns something new that opens a door to a whole new adventure? There could be amazing surprises she'd miss because she *didn't* go to the buffet."

I thought about that. Talking to Desiree at the laundry-mat had earned me a crazy friend. And it led me to Jimmy, who arranged for me to stay with Mabel. Not just one good thing, but a string of them. I could have just kept my mouth shut and walked away, but then I'd have missed all of this.

"It's an old saying, but it's true," Mabel said. "Eighty percent of life is just showing up."

I went into my room and set the imp jar before me.

"You know a lot about pain," I said to the wrigglers. "What do you think? Take the chance on a good thing, knowing it could hurt when it's gone? Or savor what happiness you can, hoping that there's other surprises down the road?"

They rippled and shimmied, but they didn't reply.

"I know one thing," I told them. "I didn't like lying to Desiree."

It was that last thought that finally brought me to Desiree's door. Mabel's borrowed satchel, filled with pajamas and such, hung over my shoulder.

I knocked. And knocked again.

I heard a giggle as the door flung open. I readied myself to grab Desiree by the arm and shout, "I can go!"—and found myself looking into a strange girl's face.

"Hi?" the girl said. She was pretty with real nice clothes, and she looked like she'd never missed a meal in her life.

"Hi. Uh. Who are you?"

"Wait, Kitty, I'm coming!" came Desiree's voice from inside the house. "I'll be right back, Ma."

And there she stood in the doorway, smiling so hard it pinked her cheeks.

"Hush!" Desiree exclaimed.

"I'm sorry. I . . ." I glanced at the plump girl. "Uh . . ."

"Oh!" Desiree threw the door open wider. "Kitty. This is my friend, Hush. Hush, this is Kitty." She waved her arms to Kitty, then me, then back again. "Kitty's coming to the fair with us. Her mother couldn't take her and—"

"She's a-spending the night?" I finished glumly.

"Yeah." A little frown creased her brow. "Are you okay? Did your plant die?"

"Her *plant?*" Kitty asked with a sniff.

Desiree turned to her friend. Her *other* friend. "Hush works at a nursery. She takes care of plants."

"Works, like a *job?*" Another sniff, and clearly a disapproving one.

"So, your plant?" Desiree said gently.

I shook my head. "No. It didn't die. It—um—wasn't as bad as I thought."

Now Desiree saw the satchel I carried. "You can come after all?" Her eyes lit up.

Kitty's eyes, I noted, did not.

I had a powerful desire to roll over Kitty like a tire over a cow pie.

"Would that be all right?" I asked.

"Yes! Come in!" Desiree pushed past Kitty and shouted toward the kitchen, "Ma! Guess what! Hush can come!"

"Yahoo!" Becky called back. Peeking her head out, she asked, "Mabel says it's okay, and all?"

"Yes, ma'am," I promised.

"Come in quick, then! Drop your things in Didi's room and we'll get gone!"

It was Jimmy and Becky, Martin and Desiree, me . . . and Kitty. The six of us piled into Jimmy's truck.

Kitty squeezed in after Desiree, so I was left to strap in

next to Martin. I gave him a smile, but he was in no mood for fun.

"I don't like rides. Cotton candy makes me puke. I don't care whose cow wins best in show," Martin complained, ticking items off on his fingers. "Why do I have to go, again?"

"Because it's your father's birthday and we're celebrating as a family," Becky replied.

Martin grunted.

"It's your birthday, Jimmy?" I called out.

"Forty-two years young," he replied.

"Well, I hope, um . . ." I'd never actually wished anyone a happy birthday before. "I hope you're even younger next year."

There was a sliver of a pause before Jimmy answered, "Thank you kindly, Hush."

In the backseat, Kitty sniffed. She was all about the sniffing, that one.

Desiree leaned forward and set her elbows on the back of the bench seat Martin and I shared. "So, tell me now! What happened with your plant? Was it a dramatic rescue?"

I turned to face her, straining against the seat belt. "Mabel said it might not be sick after all, but only in need of a new pot," I explained. "She also has this special food for transplanted plants, which is what you call it when you move them from one home to another. It has extra—"

Now watch what Kitty did here: she flat-out rolled her eyes and mouthed, *Boring.*

For Desiree's sake, I swallowed my ire and asked through gritted teeth, "Kitty, what do you do for fun?"

Desiree gave Kitty her full attention, waiting for an answer.

"I'm an equestrian," Kitty drawled.

I sifted my brain for that word and came up empty.

Desiree piped up. "That's a fancy name for a horse rider. Kitty and I take lessons together. So, I'm an equestrian, too."

"Sure," I said. "Right. A questrian."

"E-questrian." Kitty said it slow and loud, as if she was talking to a fool.

"How about some music?" Becky called from the front, then turned on the radio fairly loud.

I watched—but couldn't hear—as Desiree whispered something in Kitty's ear. *Probably talking about horses. And all their special lessons together. Kitty probably has bags of money for lessons. She probably—*

Money! Oh, crow!

"Jimmy, Becky," I yelled forward. "I'm sorry, but I left my money at Mabel's house. I have to go back for it." Would my yoga money be enough for the fair?

Ma Orr waved a hand in the air. "Oh, sugar, it's our treat."

"I don't need the charity!" I cried. "I swear if we could only just stop off—"

"Really, Hush. It's our pleasure," Jimmy shouted over the music. "It's a part of my present that we can all do this together."

My belly twisted. Charity case or ingrate? There was no way to win.

"If it's your present, I guess . . . ," I said, feeling like the poor girl headed for the rich buffet. "Thanks."

In the rearview mirror, I caught a flash of Kitty expressing her sour feelings about me. Desiree wasn't looking real happy, either.

(UN)FAIR

In the fading daylight, the sharp colors of the fair seemed magical, but treacherous, too. As if you could stare at those whirling rides and flashing neons until they held you frozen in a party-colored dream forever.

Becky disappeared, then came back with a box of gold coins. She set a handful in each of our palms: Desiree's, Martin's, Kitty's, and mine.

"I promised Jimmy we'd look at the antique cars," she told us. "Will you be all right on your own for a while?" She glanced at us, me and Kitty especially. A worried look crossed her face. "Mmm—maybe Jimmy and I should skip the cars."

Desiree's brother was already sauntering off.

"Meet us back here at nine, Martin!" Becky called after him.

"You *have* to go see the cars, Ma," Desiree told her. "Dad's been talking about it for weeks. Don't worry." She waved an arm. "We *know* most of these people."

Jimmy strode up with two race-car soda cups. "Ready, Beck?"

Ma Orr nodded. "All right. You three be good—and kind. We'll see you at nine sharp, and we'll all do the funhouse together." She wove her arm through Jimmy's and they started off. After a second, she called back to us, "Those tokens are good for food, too. Eat if you're hungry, all right?"

With that, they were gone.

I will say, I noticed one good thing right away. There wasn't a thing to steal. Food was the only thing for sale, and all the prizes were kept safe behind counters.

"What should we do first?" Desiree asked.

I set my eyes on the row of games and wondered if I could win something without cheating. "Those game booths look all right."

"Games are stupid," Kitty said. "Let's do rides."

"I think . . . we could do both," Desiree ventured, though her tone seemed a little wobbly.

As if Desiree hadn't spoken, Kitty insisted, "We *have* to go to the Tilt-A-Whirl. It's the best." She grabbed Desiree's wrist and bulldogged forward.

Desiree gave me a smile as she stumbled in the direction of the rides. "We'll do games next, Hush."

I nodded and trundled off after them. What else could I do?

The line for the Tilt-A-Whirl was thirty minutes long, and it cost each of us three tokens. For all that time and money we spent, you'd think it would be something more than getting flung in pukifying circles until they cast you out, legs a-wobbling, with a strong desire to lay down. Maybe the fair *wasn't* such a fancy buffet.

After the ride, Desiree pointed us to a ring-tossing game where you could win stuffed animals and whatnot. Desiree and I turned over a token apiece.

"I'm saving mine for something that's actually fun," Kitty sneered.

Desiree started the tossing. She didn't have very good aim, so she missed all the bottles. She did manage to knock one of the prizes off the shelf, though.

"That means she won, don't it?" I asked the attendant, knowing full well it didn't. "You ought to give it to her."

The man didn't agree, but on the glad side, my ring-tossing skills were fine. I got three out of three, which meant I could take any prize I wanted. I picked a set of jewelry pins; they matched and said "Forever Friends." Of course, I had a plan to give one to Desiree later.

After that, Kitty dragged us off to a roller coaster, then to a ride that shot a capsule of people in the air and let them fall till they almost hit the ground. I was fairly sure we were going to die, so I had to quick-decide what my dying wish was. You know, because of the way last words have special power.

As we fell into certain darkness, I whispered, "Let Nina find her way."

It turned out that we didn't die, though, so I figured Nina was on her own after all.

With all the flinging and dropping out of the way, Kitty decided it was time to eat. I couldn't fathom it. Surely her stomach was a churning mess, too! How could she even *think* of food?

I heard myself say to her, "What were you—born on Crazy Creek?"

Desiree turned pale.

A gray-red imp flared on Kitty's left shoulder. She sputtered, but found her tongue fast enough. "At least I wasn't born in a trailer! Who's doing the whiskey tango tonight? Hush Cantrell's mama in 'Bagoville, that's who!"

She didn't say anything I hadn't heard before, but the fact that she said it in front of *Desiree*? My stinger came out in a flash.

I stepped up and put my nose just an inch from Kitty's. "You keep my name out of your mouth, Madam Questrian, or I'll bring my trailer stank right to your door. You understand me?"

Kitty plainly wasn't ready for the ire I gave it. She took a step back, then another, and I could see she was afraid.

When she was a good distance off, Kitty spat, "You're *nothing*." And then, "I'm getting some food. Come on, Desiree."

Desiree looked from Kitty to me.

"Hush," she whispered, "you shouldn't have started that."

With one last, sad glance, she followed after Kitty.

And there I stood in the middle of tilts and whirls, funnel cakes and fried candy bars—with two Forever Friends pins in my pocket.

I grabbed a boy, dumped my tokens into his hands, and went to sit with the cows at the 4-H display.

Chained to a wall so they couldn't wander off, those bovines all looked as forlorn as I felt.

"You know what?" I asked one cow. "I wonder if there really are any deep-down good people after all."

It was Becky who found me collecting bits of sweet feed from where it had fallen onto the dirt floor.

"What are you doing there, Hush?" I heard her warm voice ask behind me.

"I think this cow is hungry."

I strode over and set my seed-filled hand before the cow's muzzle. She licked it up eagerly. The warmth of her tongue was a kindness, and I thought maybe I should give *her* one of the friendship pins. I could tack it to the tag in her ear.

"I see," said Becky. In a gentle mama's tone, she added, "It's after nine, you know."

I dropped my arms to my sides. "Oh, Becky. I'm sorry. I just keep messing up."

"Desiree said something happened with you three."

I nodded.

She reached out and stroked the cow. "My daddy was a cowhand. Sometimes I thought he knew cows better than he knew people."

That was something I could understand, just now. I gave a little laugh.

"He taught me some of it," she went on. "This cow, she looks healthy enough. Well fed."

"Oh. That's good."

"She may be a little sad because her baby's penned somewhere else," Becky continued. "You can see she's got a lot of milk in that udder." Now she spoke to the cow. "Are you missing your baby, sweet thing?"

The cow gave Ma Orr a lick on the chin.

"Why do people do things like that?" I wanted to know.

"Take calves from their mothers, you mean?"

I nodded. "It's cruel."

"It's"—she looked into the distance before she went on—"hard. Not every farmer does it that way."

"Did your daddy?" I asked.

She shook her head.

After a time, I said, "I don't think I can spend the night at your house."

"That's your choice." She reached around and rubbed her own back a little. I caught a glimpse of two pain imps there. "But we'd be glad to have you."

I shook my head. "Thanks, but I think I'll just walk back to Mabel's."

"It's too late for walking alone. And that's a couple miles, at least." She said it nicely, but I could tell she wasn't going to let me go off on my own.

"Please don't make me get in that truck with Kitty . . ." *And Desiree, who hates me now forever.* "Please."

"Tell you what," said Becky. "I saw JoBeth at the safety booth. Let's see if she can give us a ride, all right?"

I nodded, relieved.

"Hey, Hush?"

I looked into her eyes.

She told me, "A lot of people grow up in trailer parks. I did. And you know what that says about me, as a person? About who I am in my heart?"

I shook my head.

"Nothing," she answered.

I took that in. "Did people ever call you names?" I asked. " 'Trailer trash' and whatnot?"

"Some." She shrugged. "Nobody whose opinion I care about now. But it was hard at the time."

We were quiet for a while.

"Closing up here, ladies," the 4-H attendant told us.

I brushed dust and hay off my jeans. "I guess that means us."

Becky set an arm round my shoulders.

"She's a nice cow," I said as we walked to the safety booth.

"Very nice," Becky agreed.

144

Before she and JoBeth dropped me at Mabel's, I made sure to yank those pain imps off her back.

The next morning, I was roused by the sounds of voices. It took me a few seconds to realize that Desiree's was one of them.

I rushed onto the porch, where I found Mabel sipping tea, grinning over something Desiree was showing her.

"Hey!" I said. "Good morning!"

Desiree's smile disappeared. She took back whatever she was sharing. Two pain imps trembled near her heart.

"I'll see you later, Missus Holt." She didn't even bother to look at me as she said, "Your satchel's there on the step, Hush." And then, just to make sure I knew she wasn't doing me any favors, she added, "My ma made me bring it."

I mouthed, *Help!* at Mabel, but she only shrugged and whispered, "Talk to her!"

Meanwhile, Desiree was already down at the gate, swinging it shut behind her.

"Desiree, could you wait up? Please?" I called.

She stopped walking.

I ran up. "Hey."

"What do you want?"

I could almost hear the door of her heart as she closed it against me. My insides lurched. *Desiree and me. That was the real fancy buffet.* And now it might be over for good.

It was too soon!

I took a breath and steadied myself. I knew I had to get this right.

Unfortunately, what I said was, "Did you, uh, like the fair?"

She glared at me.

I tried again. "What was that you were showing Mabel?"

"Nothing you'd care about," she sniped.

"Please, Desiree. I'm *sorry* I didn't spend the night," I said.

She sniffed, a little too much like Kitty for my taste. "I'm glad you didn't spend the night!"

"You're . . . *glad?*" Now my temper flared. "Why, so you and Kitty could have all your separate horsey fun?"

Desiree's eyes turned to slits. "Don't you say one bad word about my horses!"

"What is *wrong* with you?" I pounded my foot. "Can't you see? That Kitty is a mean girl!"

Here's where she surprised me. "*Now* who's born on Crazy Creek? Of *course* I know she's mean!" Desiree shouted. "She's awful! But her mother gives out the scholarship that lets me do my riding lessons! If I make Kitty mad, her ma could take away the money. It could be the end of my horse riding forever!"

I was reeling over the notion of Desiree losing something so important to her, but she went on.

"But even, *even* if she's terrible—and I know she is—she was my *guest*. You should have treated her better!"

"Wait a minute now, blondie! I was your guest, too! I didn't see you get all riled up when *she* was mean to *me!*"

She crossed her arms and leaned in. "You don't know what I did or didn't do, Hush Cantrell. You left."

"I thought you were glad I didn't spend the night," I taunted.

Desiree opened her mouth, then closed it. Finally, she said, "Just leave me alone." She spun on her heel and put her back to me.

"No!" I kicked at a fencepost. "I want you to tell me why *she* is a guest and I'm—I don't even know what. The doormat under her feet, I reckon."

"*Rrrrugh!* Don't you know *anything?*" She flailed her arms wide, and I got a fresh view of those pain imps near her heart. "Guests are people to look after and tend. You're nothing like that. You're—"

"What! What am I?"

"You're—special!" Her nostrils flared, her breath came hard. "I thought you had my back! I thought you'd help me! Not make it so my fondest dream gets taken away." She dropped her chin to her chest. "Hush, I am sorry Kitty was awful to you. But I have got to be a horse witch, I've *got* to. And the teacher at the stables, she knows the way. She *knows.* If I lose that . . . I won't be me."

I felt the power of her words on my very skin. I couldn't help but believe her.

I couldn't help but put those lessons at the top of my *Get It Done* list.

"Did she? Did she take away your money?" I tried to

figure how much yoga I'd have to teach to buy horse lessons for Desiree. Or, if it came down to it, what I could steal and sell for the cash.

Desiree shook her head. "No. It's fixed, I think. My ma helped smooth everything out."

Relief flooded me. "Okay, then. So, now all we have to do is keep Kitty happy until you finish your learning." I thought for a minute. "She loves those dang amusement rides. I wonder if we could get her a ticket to Whipsaw World."

Desiree let out a little laugh. "Now you're being silly."

"I'm serious! The donation money from six or seven yoga classes should be enough. And then maybe Mabel will let us trade her the cash and she can order the ticket with her credit card and—"

She held up a hand: *Stop.*

I went quiet.

"I . . . should have told you who Kitty was. I should have told you about the scholarship," Desiree said.

"When did you have time? I showed up at your door and surprised you."

She shrugged. "But still."

"Yeah, maybe."

She reached out and pinched the fabric of my sleeve. "I did blow up at her, later. She called you a name and I blew up like a toad."

I took that in. I even tried to imagine how it might have

happened. I couldn't know for sure, of course, because no one had ever defended me before.

"You stuck up for me. That's the part your ma had to smooth over," I realized.

Desiree nodded.

I reached out for a tree branch and fiddled with a leaf. "I'm glad your lessons are safe."

She set her hand on the same tree. "Want to know something?"

"Yes, ma'am."

"Kitty snored *so* loud." She rattled a long, fake snore. "I swear, the walls shook."

I barked a laugh.

We both said sorry a few more times, and then some kind of special clouds rolled in and Desiree got all excited about that. Then I asked her if she'd come with me to check on my repotted plant. She said she would. As we hovered over the perked-up leaves, I was glad to see that Desiree's pain imps had faded to almost nothing. A little later, Mabel asked if Desiree wanted to stay for brunch—and things started to feel all right again.

I wasn't brave enough to give Desiree the Forever Friends pin face to face, but I did sneak out later that day and set it on her windowsill.

The next time I saw her, she was wearing hers and I was wearing mine, and Becky complimented us both on our good taste.

FINE

The weeks shuffled by. Before long, I learned all the names of my yoga students and even got so friendly with some of them, they'd bring me fitness clippings from their magazines. Word about the lessons spread, and things got so big that Desiree and me had to start a second class. Plus, I was getting so good at plants, people would stop by to ask *me* for help with their gardening troubles! I was getting to be a real, respected citizen!

I even found the courage to go into town now and then, to pick up something for Mabel. It seemed to both of us like a good experiment—walk in, buy what I needed, walk right back out. And it went just about that smoothly, except that everywhere I went now, I kept bumping into folks I knew. Good thing about that, it made it almost impossible to thieve. My loco seemed to figure that, too. It came around a lot less often.

Yup, everything was going real fine.

Until I saw Nina.

DUST-UP

On that particular day, Mabel had decided "the baby" positively had to have potato salad. She said that a lot, that the baby wanted something when Mabel, herself, was the one who was craving. It had become a joke between us. So I said that baby was right smart—I could surely go for some potato salad, and maybe even a burger to go with it. Then Mabel's eyes got real big and she told me what the baby *really* wanted was a cookout with burgers and lemonade and potato salad and deviled eggs! I observed that was one hungry baby, but who was I to deprive a little one? Maybe, I added, we should even invite the Orrs over, since I ain't had my mandatory family supper that week.

All this to say, we were fixin' to have a cookout.

I had a biggish grocery list, but not so much I couldn't carry it home on two arms. I'd long since learned to leave my first daddy's jacket at home when I went shopping. All that big, baggy pocketedness was nothing more than a temptation to sneak-thieve, while tiny jeans pockets could hold things I was *supposed* to carry, like dollars and change and Desiree's rock.

Mabel had tried to put some money in my hand, but I told her I'd be proud if she'd let me buy the food from my yoga dollars. Other people might not like spending the cash they earned, but for me it felt like a big ol' butt waggle in the face of my loco.

The store's ground turkey was looking a little blinky, so I asked the meat man if he could arrange something better. When he started to gee and haw, I reminded him that I was shopping for Mabel Holt—poor pregnant Mabel, having her second baby so late in life, Mabel who really did need every itty-bitty vitamin she could get, didn't he think?

Off he went, searching for better turkey, and I had nothing to do but wait. For a time, I examined a nearby potato-chip display, thinking whether "the baby" would prefer cheddar or barbeque flavor. But in the middle of that, I happened to look up, and guess who was staring right at me?

Nina had so many pain imps coming off of her, you'd have thought she'd been swimming in Leech Lake. The second our eyes locked, her frown turned to a scowl, and she started striding my way. Or she tried to. She was drunk.

"You!" She stumbled, poking a finger at me. "You ungrateful sorry excuse for a daughter! Look at you, sashaying all important-like! *Look at me! I'm a nib buying food!*" She bobbed her head in a way that, I reckoned, was meant to resemble me.

I was frozen stiff—and for stupid reasons. I had to wait on my turkey. I didn't want to make a scene. Somehow, the mere presence of my ma sucked the brain right out my head.

She got closer still, and I could smell the reek of drink on her.

"You think you're too good for me, you stupid cur? I got news for you. You're nothing! You are no-body! You're trash! And them folks you sent to mess in my business, them's no-body, too. You little—!"

I won't say the name she called me, but it was foul and cruel.

Right then, a hand thumped down on my shoulder. I nearly jumped out of my skin.

"I'd say that's about enough of that," came a familiar voice. "Time you moved on, ma'am."

I turned around and nearly melted with relief. It was Ham, my worst and most devoted yoga student. He stood behind me like a wall. Every inch of his face meant business.

"You don't know me!" Nina snarled at him, but she did begin to back away.

"Keep moving," he told her once, when she looked like she was fixin' to start up again.

And to my relief, she did. It was over.

Almost.

Nina was just about to round a corner and disappear

from sight when she shouted, "I know where you're staying!" Then she was gone.

I juddered like a plucked guitar string.

An age seemed to pass before I looked around and spied at least four people staring at me. I wasn't sure if it was better or worse that I knew two of them.

"Okay, Hush. Let's get you back to Mabel's," Ham said.

I burst into tears. It was a crazy sort of cry, loud and slobbery. The build-up of twelve years' worth of weeping, maybe.

"It's all right." Ham patted my shoulder. "You're all right. Come on, now."

"I can't!" I wailed.

"You can't?"

I shook my head. "We're having a cookout! I got to buy the meat!"

"A cookout? You got to have meat, then," he said with so much understanding I began bawling all over again.

Right then, the meat man appeared—or maybe he'd been standing there the whole time. He reached out a hand and offered me a package of turkey.

I looked it over. "That's much better." After a hard swallow, I added, "Thank you, sir."

"See? There's your meat," Ham said as gently as a three-hundred-pound man could. "Anything else you need?"

Hand shaking, I showed him my list.

He read it over. "Oh, this ain't nothing. We'll get you set up and back to your grill in no time!"

And with that, Ham Quimby led me first to produce, then to dairy. He was very kind, even carrying the handbasket up to the register for me. Then I paid for it all with my own yoga money, just like the food-buying nib my mother said I was.

When me and Ham got to Mabel's, Jimmy was already there. He and Ham disappeared round back of the house, while Mabel took the bags from my arms and led me inside.

"Are you all right, Belle?" A pain imp fluttered around Mabel's heart. I reckoned it was for me.

"You heard what happened?" I asked, alarmed.

She quirked her lip. "Living in a small town has its pros and cons. On the good side, somebody cared enough to call Jimmy, and Jimmy cared enough to call me. On the less-good side, most everybody in town will know what happened by nightfall."

I hung my head. "Ugh."

"Do you want to talk about it?"

"You said you heard it all," I told her.

"But not from you. Sometimes a person needs to say a thing out loud."

I found she was right. I told her most of it. Not all. I couldn't bring myself to say the name Nina had called me. Not because it was so rare; people in 'Bagoville said it all the time. But because it seemed so shameful to have your own ma use it on you.

155

"She said she knows where I'm staying."

Mabel sighed. "Again, no secrets in a small town."

I looked around me. Somewhere along the way, I'd begun thinking of Mabel's home as my own. On a wall, in place of pride, there hung a photo of the Holts, laughing over some private, family jest.

"Nina is my ma," I said.

"Yes, she is."

I grabbed the edge of a table. "Do you think I done her wrong, Mabel? Leaving her like that? Staying here with you, living fine?" And Nina, with all those pain imps latched onto her?

"What I think . . . wow." She looked off in one direction, then another, and shook her head. "No, Belle. I don't think you've done her wrong. I—I won't claim this isn't complicated. And hard. Goodness knows it is. But the truth is, there are certain things a person is responsible for and certain things they're not. And a kid is never, ever responsible for their parents. It's *always* the other way around. When you're old enough to make your own way in life, that can change. But for now"—she rubbed at her forehead—"Nina's done some things wrong. She's got to fix them."

"Do you think she is? Fixing them?" I asked.

"You could ask JoBeth. I think the police are checking in on her from time to time."

"She was real drunk."

"Nina? Yeah, I heard." Mabel's heart imp was bright red.

"Makes me think she might *not* be fixing things."

She was quiet for a while, sifting through her thoughts. "It's hard to say. Sometimes a person gets overwhelmed, even when they are trying. They slip up."

"But the things she said!" I cried.

"I know, Belle. The things she said."

It wasn't long before we heard Ham's truck drive away. Jimmy strode in with his own batch of imps on his heart.

"I'm sorry that happened to you, Hush," he said.

"Yeah. Thanks."

Looking at Mabel and me both, he asked, "Did y'all want to cancel the cookout? I imagine you're not in the mood for a big to-do, just now."

I spun on Mabel. "Please don't! Desiree already knows about it! Besides, I never been to a real cookout, one that ain't charitable."

Waving a hand at the room around me, I turned to Jimmy. "Someday soon this is all gonna be over. We got to cook out while the cooking's good!"

Jimmy opened his mouth, thought it over, and closed it again.

Mabel was the one who finally spoke. "We don't know what's going to happen, Belle. Not yet." Then she added, "There's no reason to cancel the party if you really want one." She smiled.

I told her I did.

Jimmy nodded and said he'd run home to collect Becky and Desiree and Martin.

After he was gone, I told Mabel, "You've got an imp over your heart, again. I—I keep bringing you pain! Don't you get tired of me?"

She set her fingertips over her chest, not far from where the imp wriggled. "Not even a little."

Recalling what she'd once said about pain having its place, I said, "So . . . I reckon you want to hold on to that one for a while, then?"

She nodded. "I think what happened to you today deserves a little grieving."

"Yeah," I whispered. "It kind of might."

After our button-buster of a supper—I learned I like my burgers well-done and smothered in onions, by the by—the grown folks gathered over coffee, Martin left to raise hell (Jimmy's words), and I took Desiree to see my favorite part of Mabel's garden. It was an old tire swing, hanging from a big oak tree, surrounded by wildflowers of every stripe.

"It's nicest if you take off your shoes," I told Desiree, one foot already bare.

She kicked off her flips. "That does feel good."

"Hop on. I'll push you," I said, standing behind the swing. "Then you dangle your toes. It's a right tickler."

She gave the tire an ambitious glance from a distance, then ran at it and threw herself on, full bore. The force of barreling-Desiree-plus-swing nearly knocked me over!

Laughing, I righted myself and grasped the swing rope. "Dog my cats, girl! You're gonna kill me!"

She laughed right back. "You didn't know I had so much power behind me!"

"I reckon I didn't!"

I gave Desiree a push, then another. Once she caught the rhythm, she leaned into it, pumping her legs to swing higher, and higher yet. I didn't know a body could climb so high on a tire swing! She just about flew. There were times, even, when it seemed she reached high as the sun, the light of it blazing all around her, turning her into something magical and wild.

After a time, Desiree stuck down her feet to help me stop the swing.

"You want a go?" she asked, breathless.

"Naw. I do it all the time." I grinned. "I like to twirl it up and let it unravel."

"That's fun," she agreed. But it seemed her voice was far off, and I thought she had something on her mind.

"The other thing I like is to lay on my belly and just hang." I said it, though I was mostly just filling the space until she chose to tell me where her mind was.

When she finally did, I wished she hadn't.

"Was that your ma in the store today?"

"You, uh, you heard about that?" I don't know why I was surprised. Mabel surely had warned me.

"Martin was in there buying a razor for his invisible beard." She was trying to lighten things up a little, but I was way past laughing. Desiree was going to know the truth of me now—maybe she already did. The end of our crazy friendship had finally come.

"Yeah," I admitted. "That was my ma."

"They say she's a hustler's shill," she told me.

"What's a shill?"

Shrug. "I thought you might know."

She was still sitting on the swing, using her feet to push her an inch this way, an inch that way.

"She's bad, though? That's why you're living with Mabel?"

I flumped down on the ground and started swatting at flower tops. "Naw. She ain't bad." I stopped to think that over. "Well, maybe she is. I don't rightly know. She's got a lot of pain imps, I did see that."

"Do you miss her?" Desiree asked.

I didn't . . . and I did. I reckoned neither answer said anything good about me. "Maybe. But I don't want to go back."

After a time, she pointed to the ground beside me. "Hand me that rock, will you?"

I did.

Squinting one eye shut, she held the rock up to the light. "Are you a thief?"

I jutted my jaw. "Word does get around, don't it?"

"Is it true?"

"It *was* true. I'm getting better." I winced a little, waiting to hear what she'd think of that.

She let the rock slip between her fingers. It hit the ground with a thump.

"Now you just steal people's pain," she mused. "Thief of pain."

"It's progress." I grinned, hoping to lead her into a smile.

"Are you really my friend, Hush Cantrell? You kept a lot of things from me." This time, when she laid those big eyes on me, it seemed she was looking at my innards, trying to suss out the truth.

It occurred to me, then, to look-see if she had a pain imp. She didn't.

"I think you probably are my friend," she went on. "But I also think you've got a few things to learn about how to be a friend."

After a time, I roused the courage to ask, "Are you *my* friend? Still?"

She reached out a foot and kicked the side of my arm. Soft-like. It didn't hurt.

"You clabberhead! You think I'd stop liking you because of who your ma is?"

Now that I thought on it, that didn't sound like something she would do.

"I reckon not," I said. "But there's the sneak thieving, too."

"But you've turned it into something good, haven't you?

Taking people's pain away?" She was silent for a time. "But—please don't ever steal from me."

I was on my feet in a shot. "I would never!"

Desiree hopped off the swing. Wrapping her arms around me from the side, and setting her cheek on my arm, she said, "And I would never stop being your friend."

DUTY

Bad dreams beat me down hard that night. First were the ones about Nina—her screaming at me in the store, her swallowing fire and puking up pain imps, her grabbing me by the hair and dragging me off while Mabel cried in a cage, belly all flat because someone stole her baby. But the worst ones were the Baron Ramey dreams. First I'd hear Nina's voice say, "I know where you're staying!" and then came Baron's, *"I know where you're staying, too!"* And there was his truck cruising that road behind Mabel's place, and I was all alone. And suddenly a door slammed in the house, and a terrible voice sang, *"The party's over!"* and the shadow of a knife appeared on a curtain—

"Wake up, Belle. It's just a dream."

The voice was gentle, but coming as it did against a back-cloth of terror, I could only run, retreating far and farther into my nightmare, looking somewhere, anywhere, for a safe place to go.

"Belle. It's Mabel. Come back now. You're all right."

The first bit of daylight snuck past my eyelids. The sleep began sloughing off. I started to recall things other than my dreams.

"Mabel?"

"Yes, honey. It's me."

Now I did open my eyes. Mabel hadn't been crying, and her belly was still fat and round.

"You—you're all right?" I asked her.

"Me? I'm fine." She nodded. Reaching off to one side, she came back with a glass of water and offered it to me.

I took it and drank deep. "Thankee."

"Welcome." After I sipped some more, she said, "Nightmares, huh? Real bad?"

"Real *real* bad," I agreed.

Recalling Mabel locked in that dream cage, seeing Baron's truck behind her dream house, and harking back to Baron Ramey's terrible song, I said, "I think I have to leave, Mabel."

"Leave? How come?"

"I'm putting you in danger. If Nina knows where I am, then Baron Ramey knows where I am, and who knows—"

"Baron Ramey? From Dietz?"

Dietz, a town not far from Sass, was known for its villainy.

"You know who he is?" I asked.

"Belle, *everyone* knows who he is. He comes into town

for the express purpose of making trouble. I think Mike Thrasher has arrested Baron Ramey more times than your— uh, your average felon." She set a piece of her hair behind her ear. "Your ma knows Baron Ramey?"

"Oh yeah," I replied. "She knows him." And all at once, I was telling the whole story about the day I got busted. About Nina's bruises and Baron Ramey's visit and their plans for me. "He is a *bad* man, Mabel. He could slip his rocker, easy, and decide to come up here and fetch me for Nina. He wouldn't think twice about hurting you to get what he wanted. You *and* the baby."

She rubbed her big belly. "I won't say it's not scary. You're right. A dangerous man like Ramey can get all kinds of nastiness under his skin. But it's a small town, and when I let Sheriff Thrasher—and JoBeth, and Jimmy, and Ham— know Baron Ramey's in the picture, I have no doubt the wrath of all Sass will rain down *long* before Baron gets within a hundred paces of this house."

"But—"

Mabel held up her hand. "Remember what I was saying just yesterday, about how it's always the adult's responsibility to look out for the kid?"

"Yeah."

"Let me do my job, girlfriend. You stay right here and let all us grown-ups do our jobs."

One part of me wanted to argue, but another part of me thought, *What would that be like, to be taken care of, to be kept*

165

safe? The answer gave me such a snug feeling that I wanted to burrow into it and hide from my old life forever.

The argufying part won a little. "But Baron Ramey's smart!"

"No, Belle. Baron Ramey is strong and fractious and mean. But he is *not* smart." She seemed to be thinking hard when she added, "I do want you to be careful when you're going around town, though. Stay where people can see you. Try not to be alone. You hear me?"

"Yes, ma'am," I replied.

"Hang in there, Belle. Maybe go sit in a patch of sunlight to chase away the last of those nightmares. There's breakfast on the table and fresh buttermilk in the fridge. Eat your fill. I'm going to phone the cavalry."

"Yes, ma'am."

She left to make her calls.

You'll likely never hear me say this *ever* again, but sometimes it's downright comforting to let an adult lay down the law.

• • •

While I was feeling fairly *safe* with every eyebulb in town upon me, having each person in Sass know my personal business was no bowl of Monkey Puffs.

Oh, sure, I got plenty of sympathy: "It just breaks my

heart to think of you cooped up in that dirty motor home with that wicked mama of yours!"

And, as one might imagine, it was hard not to be grateful for well-meant help such as: "It ain't your fault your ma's a reprobate. You just hold your head up high!"

I got legal advice, too: "What you got to do is put a ad in the *Sass Settee*, saying you're officially severing yourself from all your mama's affairs. That way, if she robs a bank or something, you're not liable for the money."

After a week of scrutiny and counsel, I was feeling so vexed that my loco got the best of me. Desiree and me were looking at the magazines at Beezer's when the pressure come on so hard and so fast I had a borrowed gum pop in my pocket afore I even knew it.

"Hush!" Desiree whispered.

"What?"

She flared her nostrils and pointed at my hip.

I looked down to see the paper stick poking out my pocket.

"Aw, crap."

Worser still, Peggy the shopkeep was standing right there and saw the whole thing!

I walked up to the woman and offered her the gum pop. Head hanging low, I said, "I'm terrible sorry, ma'am."

Peggy took my face in her hands. "You keep it, sugar. I know your life ain't been all grits and cheese."

It took all my manners not to *grit* my teeth as I thanked her.

"C'mon, Desiree," I said, tugging my friend's arm. "Let's go! I reckon I need to go reflect on what I done."

Outside, the sky was threatening rain.

"I am running out of patience for the Poor, Pathetic Hush Sympathy Squad!" I ranted once we were out of earshot of the store.

"They mean well," Desiree said.

"Course they mean well!" I exclaimed. "But which is worse? Pity or scorn? I ain't so sure! Do you know what one lady said to me yesterday? She told me she was praying for my ma to go to prison! What's a body to make of that?"

"Was it Missus Sweeney?"

"Yeah! How'd you know?"

"She prays for Martin to go to prison, too," Desiree told me. "Says it'll straighten him out."

I laughed. "All right. Well. At least I ain't alone, then."

A car door slammed. "Belle? Desiree? Is that you, girls?"

We looked up. Everly Binset, one of our yoga students, was headed our way.

"I'm so glad I ran into you two!" She looked a frazzle. Her pinned-up hair had come undone on one side, and a smear of jelly marred the SUMMER FUN scrubs she was wearing.

"Into *us* two?" I asked as she caught her breath. "Why?"

Now that she stood in front of us, I could see that she was wilted as a sun-beaten flower.

"You know I run the old folks' home—"

I hadn't known, but Desiree nodded.

"Well, the Pitney kids' choir was driving over today to entertain my seniors, but their bus broke down and they can't make it. To make things worse, two of my nurses are out sick, so we don't have anyone else to lead activity hour, either. So I'm wondering if you two, out of the goodness of your hearts, might . . . ?"

It took me a second to catch on. "You want us to sing to your old people?"

She gave us a tight smile. "Sing. Tell jokes. Whatever you could do. I'd really appreciate it."

"I guess we could teach them yoga," Desiree ventured. "But they probably can't get down on the floor, can they?"

I considered that. "They're too fragile, I bet. But you know what old people do like?" In my mind's eye, I saw the poster in Crispy's room, how he'd hung it so proudly. "Art to hang on their walls, things that will cheer them up. Everly, do you have any old magazines we could cut up?"

"Oh, yes. Tons of them," she replied.

I poked Desiree's shoulder. "I think we ought to teach them to make treasure maps."

Her mouth formed a glad O. "That's perfect!" Turning to Everly, Desiree said, "We'd need glue and scissors, too."

169

"We've got safety scissors and glue sticks aplenty," the woman told us.

"All right!" Helping folks make treasure maps was better than hiding from neighbor pity any day. "See you there?"

"Yes! Give me thirty minutes to run an errand and dig out the supplies!" She was off and running again. Over her shoulder, she called, "I've got prescriptions to pick up!"

By the time we got to the seniors' home, Everly had the magazines and scissors ready for us. The elders gathered in the recreation hall, seated in chairs—some of them even belted in. They had a flurry of pain imps among them, so I was glad we'd come.

Before I could start plucking imps, though, I had to put them to work on their maps. I stood up at the front of the room, gave everyone a friendly grin, and began to explain.

"Now, a treasure map is where you pick out things you want to bring into your life."

Desiree chimed in, too. "Things you dream of, or maybe something you'd like to become. Just look at the magazines and see what inspires you."

"Then you cut out the pictures, glue them on, and later you can look back to see if your treasures came to you." I gave a nod to let them know I was done.

A long stretch of quiet followed. Nobody picked up a magazine or a scissors.

"Were we talking too soft?" I asked Desiree.

She shrugged.

Standing on my tiptoes, I hollered, "A TREASURE MAP IS WHERE YOU PICK OUT THINGS—"

"We heard you fine, sugar," one lady told me. "We just don't have much in the way of big plans."

"If you got a picture where Nurse Binset *isn't* poking me with a needle, I'll cut that out!" said another.

A few folks chuckled.

I gave the rest home a hard look, taking in the long hall of doors, the drone of the television in the corner. Truth to tell, it *didn't* seem the sort of place where things liked to change.

At the same time, I couldn't believe these folks just wanted to sit around, all quiet and still, until the hospice bus came for them.

"Well, maybe it isn't so much about what you want for the future, as . . ." I trailed off. Something was tickling the tip of my brain, but how could I get to it?

Looking at all those wrinkled faces, I found myself thinking of Crispy. "Look here. My friend Crispy, he's gonna die. But instead of getting all cross-legged about it, he looks forward to the people he'll see on the other side. And he thinks of ways to spread kindness before he goes.

"You folks, you've got *lots* more time than he does," I told them. "If I were you, I'd spend it like Crispy does. Looking for

171

little pieces of goodness you can do. Help you could bring. Maybe you could cut out pictures of that."

"If you haven't noticed," a man called from his wheelchair, "my helping days are over. *I'm* the one who needs the help now."

The man's friend nodded, but other folks had troubled looks, as if that notion didn't set well with them.

"She is right about one thing," said a woman with an armful of knitting. "We're not exactly serving our fellow man, are we?"

"I wasn't finding fault—" I tried to say.

But she went on, "Look at me. I eat three square meals a day. I've got a roof over my head. *And* I've got hands that can knit. Meanwhile, I guarantee *somebody* in this county will need a warm scarf or a sweater, come winter." She patted the chubby lady next to her. "Someone could surely use one of your shawls, Wanda. Nobody crochets like you do."

"I've got six of them just sitting in my closet," Wanda agreed. "It does seem like a waste."

"I remember, my husband and I had some lean years," one of the seniors mused. "No money to fix the heater. Cold as all get-out. A neighbor brought us some heavy coats, a couple extra blankets. It meant so much to us."

"I wonder if we could get all our sewing together," Wanda said, "box it up—"

"Start a clothes drive, even." The knitting lady sat up straighter. "Get everybody to turn their knitting needles to the greater good. I bet my niece would make us a bunch of baby booties."

Wanda tapped a finger on the table in front of her. "We could cut up these magazines to make posters. Put them up along Main Street." She waved her arms, forming an imaginary poster on a wall. "'Knit for Your Neighbors! Crochet for the Kids!'"

"I can just see it now!" exclaimed the man in the wheelchair. "You two hobbling along Main Street, posting notices. You can't even take a shower without help!"

"You don't know nothing about me and my shower," Wanda shot back.

Desiree and I, who had been all but forgotten, shared a look. These seniors had started a good ball rolling. All we had to do was give it a nudge.

I told the elders, "We'll hang your posters."

"And once the fancywork gets collected," Desiree said, "I know my parents would drive it to Hope House."

Hope House was a place where needy people got sacks of food or clothes and such. Nina used to make me go there and pretend I wasn't her daughter so we could beat the one-bag-per-family rule.

"Mabel would help, too, I bet," I added.

Now other folks piped up. One fellow thought the *Sass Settee* would print an ad for free. Plus, he offered a bunch of home-knit socks he wasn't wearing anymore.

"I'm a full-time slippers man, these days," he explained.

The knitting lady wrapped it all together and set a bow on top: "The first annual Sass Retirement Home 'Knit for Your Neighbors' clothing drive."

"Wouldn't that be a peach?" one of the elders marveled.

"Come on now, people," Wanda hollered. "If you don't knit, you can still make posters."

Now the old folks tore into those magazines like you wouldn't believe. Scissors raced across the page! Paper scraps went a-flying!

Desiree tacked up a paper listing the things that would need to go on every poster: the address of the nursing home, the dates and times when people could drop off donations.

Meanwhile, I headed for a lady who was wincing from the effort of working her scissors. Strangely, there wasn't a single pain imp on her hands.

"Hurts?" I asked her.

"No," she replied. "Just stiff. It's good for me to move them."

I couldn't help admiring her persistence.

Next, I made my way over to a little old man, one of the belted-in ones. He hadn't raised his scissors, nor had he taken a magazine. I wasn't surprised. He was so covered in pain imps, I could hardly see the person underneath.

Real careful, I helped him open a copy of *Georgia Style*. It was a good chance to brush imps off his sides, too. Then I pretended to drop the scissors so I could get the imps off the man's feet. They were especially bad there. A few minutes later, his whole body seemed to soften, and he began letting out one sigh after another. His relief was so wholehearted, it was almost painful to hear.

By the end of the hour, I'd stopped at everyone's table and sneak-plucked all the imps I could find. I even had to take a cup from the nurses' station to hold them. From the bulk of the class, I'd gathered maybe twenty. From the belted-in man, all by himself, I had another forty of them, easy.

Nobody made a treasure map, but everyone seemed lively and glad. Those seniors gave Desiree and me twenty posters to hang! Everly fed us cookies and punch and told us we were welcome to come back anytime—especially later that week if Amy the Calisthenic Lady couldn't make it in.

Desiree took her cookies and sat at a tableful of ladies who were talking about the RNN.

"They have some new shows next season that'll really surprise you!" I heard her say.

Me, I sat beside my little man—called Nate—whose face had gone soft and smiling with the lack of imps. I thought he might fall asleep soon. It was easy to imagine life was a real uphill battle living with all of those imps stuck to you. Cut forty of them buggers loose, and I might be ready for a nap, too.

As I was munching a cookie, Nate whispered something I couldn't hear.

"What's that, sir?" I leaned in to listen.

"I say, my granny used to do what you done."

"Your granny helped folks make art?"

He gave a faint shake of the head. "Naw. Pain lifting. Like you done."

It took me a second to understand what he was telling me. I'd been so sure I was alone.

"You—you mean I'm not the only one?" I stammered.

Though Mabel had talked about Sass shines, I surely hadn't expected *this*. A kindly elder who'd come before me, a lady not so different from gentle Nate, here? I was a little sad I'd never get to meet her.

Speaking softly into Nate's ear, I asked, "I don't reckon you recall any of her good wisdom?"

He was quiet for so long I thought he'd drifted off. But his lips started moving again and he told me, "She did say she felt pain was a teacher, and we should heed it."

I gave that a think. "I don't rightly know what that means, Mister Nate."

"You're a good girl," was all he said.

Then he did fall asleep, for real. But he was still grinning ever so slightly, and I felt mighty fine just sitting there, watching him rest.

The peacefulness on Nate's face stuck with me all day, and for much of that time I was so pleased to have helped him.

But as the hours passed, something else snuck up on me. An unease, I guess you'd call it. Nina kept popping up in my mind.

That had been *my own ma* I'd seen staggering drunk through Sass Foods, her heart all blown out with pain imps! Not to mention the other dozen or so hanging off the rest of her. What's a girl—what's a *daughter*—to do with that?

It made it hard to concentrate on my gardening. I ended up planting a whole packet of parsley seeds in the radish tray. Later, at dinnertime, I had trouble keeping up with Mabel's talk about some funny thing or other that happened at the Women's Club meeting. And when we turned on a movie, I know there were places I was supposed to laugh, but the jokes just zoomed right by me.

Finally, around nine, I gave up and went to bed.

I dreamed I was back in that old folks' home, and there was Nate after I'd plucked the pain imps off of him, looking so content, just about to say I was a good girl. All at once, though, he began to turn inside out, like he was being sucked inside himself, slipping, roiling, until—there Nina appeared in his place, strapped to the chair.

"I'm dying," she moaned, though it wasn't her normal voice, but rather the sound she'd make if she was underwater, fixin' to drown. "I'm dying of pain!" Blood-red imps spilled from her mouth.

Two more nights went by, the same dream over and over, but with more imps each time. Mouthful after mouthful they poured out, until the world turned red in a deluge of pain. Nearly every hour it woke me up, leaving me shaky, heart a-pounding.

On the fourth night of it, two-thirty a.m., I sat bolt upright in bed.

"I know!" I whisper-shouted at my old jar of pain imps and another, bigger one beside it.

No, I wasn't supposed to visit Nina. And, no, it surely wasn't safe to go anywhere Baron Ramey might be. But my mother was dying of her suffering and here I was, the very *thief* of pain, doing nothing!

How could I let that stand?

CATASTROKE

Mabel said the sheriff's office had promised to drive by every half hour or so, and they were as good as their word. I huddled in a patch of garden shadow, waiting for the car to make its rounds—then I got gone.

I made my way from one clump of dark to the next, sneaking past houses and across pastures. A cow lowed as I passed by; I reckoned she was nervous for her baby.

The walk seemed longer than I remembered. 'Bagoville was pitch-black, but my eyebulbs had rejiggered themselves for nighttime seeing. Creeping as quietly as I could, I wended my way past the junk, then circled around our RV to be sure there wasn't any sign of Baron Ramey or some other guest. Nina was alone.

I picked the door lock and slipped inside my house.

The smell of it hit me first. Yeah, the place was stank from unwashed clothes and mildew and a black-water leak. But the curious thing was, underneath all of that nastiness, there was the scent of something else—of me and Nina combined. It was home.

A hurtful, twisting sensation gripped me in my center.

As I passed by the dingy mirror on the outside of the half-closet, I saw myself fairly lit up with pain imps. When I looked down at myself, though, they were gone, just like before.

Ain't nothing I can do about that, I figured.

Nina was sound asleep on the bed in the back of the motor home, just a deadweight, not snoring or thrashing around at all. The imps had her good, though, and I wondered if they soured her dreams.

There being no time like the present, I climbed up on the bed and started plucking pain imps off of my mother. I'd worn my first daddy's jacket on purpose, knowing it would be faster just to shove imps in my pockets rather than fiddle with a jar.

It took me less than a minute to get them all.

Nina hadn't so much as stirred. I couldn't even tell if having those imps off of her gave her any real relief. In a way, though, it didn't matter. I'd done what I could. And no matter what Mabel had said, I did believe I was responsible for Nina in this one way. Wasn't I the only person, after all, who could pluck those imps? Surely she couldn't have done it for herself.

———

I took care to lock the door behind me and was glad to see the outside darkness was still unbroken. Sneaking back was easy enough, and I even stopped to pat the cow calf on my way back through the pasture.

Back on Mabel's road, I glanced one way, then the other to be sure no lawman's car was coming. There wasn't, so I let myself in at the gate.

Every light in the house was on! The sheriff's cruiser sat in the garden, doors flung open, radio squawking. There was Ham's truck and Jimmy's truck, both parked crazy-wise as if they'd pulled in at a rush.

The front door flew open. Mabel rushed out.

"Jim, I refuse to just sit here while—" She turned and saw me.

Squinting into the shadows, she said, "Belle? Honey? Is that you?"

I gulped. "Yes, ma'am."

"Thank God!" And just like that, her arms were around me and she was kissing the top of my head and patting at my arms like she was checking to be sure I was all right. "Belle! What happened? Where have you been? Ramey didn't—?"

I steeled myself for the worst, by which I mean the truth. "No. It wasn't nothing to do with Baron. I, uh—"

Now the men stepped out on the porch. When they saw me there, they came running. Just in time to hear me say—

"I was over at Nina's."

The ruckus that followed was bad enough, full of *whats*

and *whys*. But when it became clear that I'd gone there by my own free will, the upscuddle turned awful.

"Oh, Belle!"

"You made a promise!"

"What were you thinking?"

"Obviously, she wasn't thinking, Mike!"

The worst of all came from Mabel, though, when she asked the men, "Well, what did you expect?"

As if I was some kind of trailer-trash washout just destined to fail her!

A switch flipped in me.

"I'm Nina Cantrell's girl, don't you know!" I roared. "Surely any reason I had for going there was wicked and wrong! Oh, if only I had listened to you good, upstanding folk! If only I weren't so despisable and rotten to the core! What hope was there *ever* for sneak-thieving, *repro*bate little Hush Cantrell?"

They stared slack-jawed, all of them. Finally, Mabel looked as if she was about to find her voice, but I didn't want to hear it.

"And by the by!" I shouted, snatching a pain imp off the side of Ham's belly as I stormed past. "I thought there weren't no penalty for honesty in this house!"

With no place else to go, I locked myself up in my room. Which, of course, wasn't my room, but someone else's. It had only been a game of pretend all along, the idea that I could be something different. Something more.

What did you expect?

The next day, Desiree and I were supposed to teach a yoga class, but I wasn't in any kind of mood for it.

Mabel looked up from her breakfast as I entered the kitchen, but I sailed right past her and headed for the phone.

"Everly? This is Hush. Ain't no yoga today."

"Laura Lynn? This is Hush. Ain't no yoga today."

"Skeeter? This is Hush. Ain't no—"

The call-waiting chimed. I clicked over.

"Mabel Holt's house, Garden Assistant speaking," I snarled.

"It's Sue, sugar! Put Mabel on!"

Even though I was mad, I knew real strain when I heard it, so I handed the phone over right quick.

Surprised, Mabel set the telephone to her ear. "Hello?"

As she listened, a deep red pain imp flared over her heart. Her face turned pale. "What? How? I only just saw him last night! Aren't there supposed to be, I don't know, warning signs?" She cupped her hand over her heart. "Bless him. I'll be right there!"

"What happened?" I asked, my ire forgotten.

She was already running for her keys. "Ham's appendix burst! He's very sick."

"Are you going to the hospital?" I asked as she flew by me.

"Yeah!" she called back.

"Wait up, then!"

Without the radio on, the jangle of the truck's keys against the steering column was downright harsh.

"Could he die?" I asked as we drove.

Mabel gave a long blink and blew out a breath. "Yes."

I don't know how many of us there were, crowded in that waiting room. At least twenty. Besides me, Mabel, and Sue, the Orrs were there, plus JoBeth, a couple yoga students, Peggy from Beezer's, and a whole slew of people whose faces I was learning to recognize but couldn't yet name. As the bunch of us sat around, waiting on news, another family filed in.

"How is he?" the mother asked.

Even Sue's shrug was exhausted. "We're waiting."

Mabel got up to go rub Sue's shoulders, so the chair next to me turned empty. Desiree came over, sat down, and took my hand. She didn't say anything, but I reckon we had reached a place in our friendship where words weren't always needful.

We were still holding hands when a nurse came into the room.

Sue stood up. "How is he, Lainey?"

"He's out of the woods," the nurse replied with a little smile.

A great wave of relief surged out over the room. More

than one person's heart imp turned pale, and a couple even winked out.

"Lain, can you tell us anything?" Mabel asked. "Isn't this the kind of thing a person sees coming?"

The nurse held up her empty hands. "Usually, yeah. You'd expect a whole *lot* of pain before an appendix ruptures! It's the body's early-warning system—a signal to get help *before* things turn dangerous. But Ham said he didn't feel much of anything. Just a sharp twinge last night, then it passed. Gone as quick as it came."

My hands began to tremble. My whole insides quivered.

"Desiree," I whispered. "Where's your appendix?"

She pointed to a spot on the bottom right side of her belly.

Right where I'd nabbed that pain imp off Ham last night!

Pain is a teacher. That's what old Nate's granny taught. And what did a teacher do but give you help—and yap at you when you were going astray?

No, no, NO! *I* done it to Ham! *I* took away his early-warning system! He didn't feel no pain, so he didn't get no help! His appendix just got bigger and bigger until it blew up! He could have died—because of me!

"Hush, what's wrong?" Desiree asked. "Didn't you hear? Nurse Cussler says Ham's gonna be all right!"

I shook my head. "You don't understand."

"Understand what?" She gripped my hand tighter than before. "Tell me."

"I can't. I gotta—" I pulled away from her. "I gotta go!" I ran off to the bathroom and very nearly puked up *my* appendix.

I don't think anyone figured out I was behind Ham's appendix busting, and I sure didn't tell no one. If folks thought I was trouble before, what would they make of me now that I'd nearly killed someone?

Life turned fairly grim. A bunch of storm clouds rolled into town and stayed, leaving the skies bruised with a rain that threatened but never broke. And me, I started shutting folks out, not talking to Mabel or Desiree, locking myself in my room, eating alone, stewing. Sometimes I'd do nothing but sit and look at the pain imps, picking up the jar and setting it down again, wondering, What could I—what *should* I—have done different?

From desolation to anger I flew. I was madder than I was the night I came back from Nina's, everyone so disappointed in me. Madder, I think, than all the times I'd been mad in my life, combined. I was rageful mad at that Bigger Power they made such a big deal about in Jimmy's *Big Book*.

"What was I supposed to do? Let them suffer?" I shouted Upward. But just then my words took a turn and swirled around my head a few times. "Hold up! I must be addled, asking You! *You* leave people to suffer all the time! Bigger Power? Ha! Mighty right! Bigger Power to do nothing!" I picked up the *Big Book*. "Oh, Bigger Power! It's a good thing we have you! Whatever would we do without all your most excellent helping?"

I lobbed that book across the room and left it where it landed, open facedown with pages bent.

"I hate you!" I screamed up at Bigger Power.

BROKEN

And there I was. Back where it all began. Staring at the candles in Beezer's.

The light that come in through the front windows was dingy. Folks passed by, heads ducked down, collars up, as if a rain was falling.

I was wearing my first daddy's jacket. My loco was up, keen and primed. And I knew, guaranteed, I weren't gonna get caught today. When I really cranked my engine, all pistons firing, I was just too darn good.

A woman ducked into the store. Her cheeks were streaked with tears and she was looking for some kind of medicine for her baby.

"He won't stop crying! With Tad off working, and me being sick all the time! Sue's got him right now, but, Peggy, you got to help me!" Pain imps flared all along the right side of her head.

But I wasn't worried about pain imps. The shopkeep had her hands full. That's all I cared about.

My eyes were on the finest of the candles, the shimmering gold ones. Their wrappers said they were scented like Christmas.

I slipped two of them into my jacket, then took a third. All at once, though, I thought better of it, put the candles back in their box—and pinched the whole case instead. Twelve golden candles.

Drunk on loco, I rearranged the display so it looked like nothing was missing. A mighty fine job, and I said so myself.

With my jacket puffed up around me, and my arm cradling the box just so, I left Beezer's without so much as a backward glance.

But I wasn't finished yet.

Under those useless, rainless skies, I crossed Main Street, turned down Swift, and made for a pair of white double doors.

FIRST CHURCH OF SASS, said the fancy plaque on the wall.

I snatched the pen from the guest book and strode down that center aisle to the big altar up front.

There wasn't anything convenient to lean against, so I knelt down on one of the steps and set the box on my knees. Uncapping the pen, I wrote on the lid, *A present, BP. Thanks for all your great help!*

I proceeded to break every one of the candles.

Real careful-like, I put the broken pieces—every last bit of wax—in the box. I shut the lid, and set the whole package next to the cup on the altar.

On my way out, I stopped to write in the guest book. *Nina Cantrell's girl—'Bagoville.*

Then I went to the police station to turn myself in.

EMERGENCY

A dispatcher called Jimmy and Mabel. JoBeth wasn't there, so they called her, too. The sheriff was in some kind of meeting, but he radioed to say he'd be there soon—*and not to let me go nowhere.*

Fine by me. I sat in that chair, arms folded, and waited.

Mabel was the first to arrive. She had two new pain imps over her heart. I turned my eyes aside from those.

"Are you all right?" she asked.

"Fine," I told her.

"I brought you a muffin. You didn't eat before you . . . left."

"Not hungry."

Jimmy came in. "Are you all right?" he asked.

"Fine," I told him.

"Desiree sent you this." He held out a folded piece of paper.

I very nearly took it.

"Don't want it."

He pocketed the note. Turning to the dispatcher, he asked, "Mind if we use the room down at the end of the hall?"

"Be my guest," said the man.

JoBeth appeared just as we were getting settled, so now we were four. Five if you counted the flying duck pictured on the wall.

"What happened, Hush?" Jimmy asked.

"I stole some candles. Then I broke 'em. Then I left 'em in the church."

"Yes, we know," Mabel said. "But what *happened?*"

I couldn't decide what to tell them. I knew I was going to juvie; that much was plain. But did I want to go there on a charge of thieving—or one for near-murder, seeing as how I'd almost killed Ham? A brain-cousin of my loco asked, *Why tell them anything at all?* They'd only hear what they expected to hear—a poor excuse from a trashy girl who don't know any better.

Mabel's eyes shone with tears. Her imps burned scarlet.

Two wrongs don't make a right, I recalled hearing sometime in my past.

Justice ain't for poor folk. I'd heard that, too.

Finally, I shut my eyes and said, "It was my fault Ham got sick."

Jimmy made a hissing sound and leaned back in his chair.

"What do you mean, your fault?" Mabel wanted to know.

I tried to remember how angry I'd been, recalling Mabel's terrible words, *What did you expect?* But Mabel's heart was on her sleeve. So, I started piecing together the story for them—for her, mostly. I had just come to the part where I'd plucked the pain imp off Ham's belly, when jingling keys and heavy footsteps sounded in the hall. Sheriff Thrasher appeared in the doorway.

"Folks." He nodded.

"Hey, Mike," Mabel said softly.

The sheriff set his thumbs into his belt. "We got us a situation."

The adults disappeared for a time. Only Mabel came back.

She sat down in her same chair and put a cup of water before me. I took a few sips before she spoke.

"Something's happened to Nina," she told me.

As I say, I know real strain when I hear it. Water sloshed over the rim of the cup as I dropped it onto the table. "What?"

"Someone . . . beat her up. She's in the emergency room—"

I was out of my chair in a flash. "Will you take me?"

She said she would.

———

It was a terrible sort of familiar, that drive to the hospital, the second time in a week. Mabel was mostly quiet. I asked if Nina could die.

"I don't think so," she replied.

"All right." I blew out a big breath. "All right."

As she pulled into the parking space, Mabel said, "Can I say one thing before we go in?"

"Hurry," I told her, my hand already on the door handle.

"This is not your fault."

But I knew from the very fact that she said it at all—it surely was.

The room's window curtain had been pulled shut, but Sheriff Thrasher opened it before he'd let me go in alone.

The light was harsh and the coldish air smelled like medicine. Nina sat upright on her bed, one arm in a sling, the other hand fiddling with the tips of her hair. She looked up when I came in.

"Hush?" she asked as if she didn't expect to see me there.

I quick-counted a dozen new pain imps on her.

"Yeah," I said.

"But we ain't allowed to see each other."

"Sheriff said it was all right."

"Oh." She nodded. I made out a bruise on her far cheek. Her eyes were darker than normal, too. Not blackened like they'd been hit, but sunken, like she was pulling inside herself—or fixin' to sneak out the back door of her mind.

"Was it Baron?" I asked.

Again, she only nodded.

Where had the angry rebel Nina gone? She should have been swearing six ways from sideways, furiously shaking her head and slapping at walls. She should have been swearing off Baron for good (not that it would last) and telling me to mind my own beeswax.

I couldn't take her unnatural quiet. "Are you gonna tell me what happened or not?"

"I would if I could," she replied. "I don't rightly know."

"What do you mean, you don't know?" Had he given her something? Like a drug? My hackles rose.

"It was . . . the most curious thing," she said. "Couple days, maybe a week ago, I woke up feeling so strange. Like I had been locked up in a cage, but suddenly I was free." She dipped her chin, then winced as a pain imp on her neck went from pale to dark red. "*Ye-ah*. Like I'd been in a body-shaped cage, steel all around me, right up against my skin." She wrapped her good hand gingerly around the slung-up wrist, to show me. "But I didn't know it was there until it was gone." She smiled, though a smile on her was so rare, it hung a little strange on her face. "It was gone!"

It didn't take a rocket scientist to figure she was talking about the morning after I'd plucked her pain imps.

"And I was feeling so good," she went on. "Started cleaning the place up. Thinking of ways I might convince the sheriff to let you come home. Caught a notion that I ain't been a real good ma—" A pain imp over her heart flashed deep red.

She drifted off for a time.

"Baron turned up this morning. Real early. Like, four. He was drunk. And angry. And all of a sudden, I thought, I can't have this in my home! I can't have this in my life! I am a person!" Her eyes were wide with wonder. "I said that to him! Can you believe that? *I am a person!* Then I told him to get out of my house.

"He didn't like that none. So he—" She turned her cheek out where I could see it better. She held up her broken arm. "Lucky he didn't do worse, I reckon."

I stood there staring. I'd lifted Nina's pain—and what had come of it? She sassed back at Baron Ramey and he broke her arm!

My feet started moving toward the door.

"I got to go," I heard myself say. "Hope you feel better soon."

Mabel found me in the hallway. "You all right, Belle?"

I shook my head.

"Am I allowed to come back home with you?" My voice sounded a million miles away.

"Absolutely." Hers wasn't much closer.

"I'd like to go there now, if we could. Please."

After the fact, Mabel told me I'd slept for a day and a half. There weren't any pain imps in my dreams this time. No Baron Ramey, either. But I did keep seeing those candlesticks I borrowed. Except, instead of gold wax, they were real, solid gold. And when I snapped them in two, they let off a fine golden powder that stuck to my hands and wouldn't brush off.

The rules were different after that. I didn't have to go to juvie, but Mabel and Jimmy made me sit down with them for a half hour each day to talk about things. Not any particular things. Whatever I wanted to talk about, in fact. But I had to talk.

I was also on a sort of restriction. For the time being, I wasn't allowed to go anywhere alone. It didn't matter who I was with—it could be Desiree or Mabel or the man in the moon—but I couldn't go around by my lonesome.

There was one other punishment I added for my own self, mostly because I was mad and determined to make myself learn. I was gonna read that *Big Book* and study about all the ways my loco made me crazy. Because it seemed to me that far worse than the sneak thieving of flosses and candlesticks was the stealing of pain imps—a crime that just about got two people killed. No, I didn't care much for that Bigger Power they was so excited about in that hardcover, but the *Big Book* was 575 pages long. The BP couldn't be on every single one of them, could it?

The book was still turned facedown on the carpet in my room.

"See, this is what you get," I said to myself as I turned it over and unbent the folded pages. "Now you have to read."

I read.

We took inventory, making a list of all that was good, and all that was bad, about us. For the first time, we saw ourselves clearly. With clarity came courage. We asked our Higher Power to help us make amends for each of our wrongs. That was when things really began to change.

When things really began to change, huh? Change, I reckoned, was exactly what I needed to do. For starters, I needed to stop putting folks in the hospital with my pain thieving.

I skipped over the Bigger Power stuff and honed in on that word *amends*.

"What's amends?" I asked Jimmy that night as he and me and Mabel sat around the table.

His eyebrows shot up. "You been reading that book I gave you?"

I nodded.

"Good for you. All right." He set his hand on his chin and appeared to think it over. "An amends is a way to make something right. If you owe money, you try to pay it back or work it off. If you owe an apology, you give it."

Suddenly, the engine in my brain sparked and roared to life. I turned to Mabel. "Like Crispy did with his letter?"

She nodded. "Yes, actually."

Jimmy didn't know what we were talking about, so I told him about Crispy.

"That's a fine amends," Jimmy agreed.

"Did you ever make amends?" I asked him.

"I made a lot of them, after I quit drinking."

I thought back to Nina in the grocery store and all the apologies she might owe. And that was just the one time; she wasn't even a regular drinker. A full-on drunk really could have a heap of amends to make. "Was it hard?"

He sipped from a coffee mug. "It was at first. But then it started to feel really good."

21

AMENDS

"Desiree, will you help me with something?"

The rainless clouds had gone, leaving the sky summer bright. We were sprawled out on the Orrs' front lawn, soaking wet from helping wash Jimmy's truck, then turning the hoses on each other. Desiree was in her bathing suit, but I didn't have one, so I wore some old shorts and a top of Mabel's that read I DIG NATIVE PLANTS!

"You know I will," she replied. "What's up?"

Desiree knew pretty much everything now. I'd told her about how my imp plucking had harmed Ham and Nina. She also knew about me stealing the candlesticks and what I'd done with them. Her eyes turned wide and worried as I explained about Baron—from the breaking of Nina's arm to the time he'd held me to a wall by my throat, which I'd never told anyone before. But even after all that . . . I could tell Desiree still liked me just fine.

I said, "Okay, so you know I'm trying to bust out of my loco for thieving, right?"

"Right."

"Well, I'm reading this book your dad gave me—at first I stole it, but then he said I could keep it—and it says, if I want to change, I have to do some things."

She rolled onto her side and pushed herself partway up on her elbow. "Like what?"

I turned, too, so we were facing each other. "I have to make a list of myself, everything good and everything bad about me. Then, when I see all the things I've done wrong, I have to go around and make stuff right."

"Okay," she said.

"Yeah, but you don't understand. I've done a *lot* of things wrong. Just keeping track of it all is gonna be a chore!"

She sat upright now. "It won't be as hard as you think. I'll even do it with you."

"You'd do that?" I asked. "Make a list, too?"

Desiree dipped her chin. "We can plunk it into my tablet and make it all official."

"And your computer can tell us which amends to make?"

"It can tell us what we've done and what's left to do," she replied.

I grinned. "All right, then! Let's dump out the trash cans and polish the silver, girl! We're cleaning house!"

"I'm a sneak thief and an occasional fabler. I do stuff without thinking first. I quit school, and even when I did go, I was late a lot. I've been selfish and rotten, and most days I'm at least a little ornery. You got all that?" I asked, looking over Desiree's shoulder at her computer tablet.

Ornery, she typed. "Okay, yeah. But you haven't named a single *good* thing about yourself."

"All right. I'm—" I ransacked my brain. Twice. "I can't think of anything."

Desiree shook her head and rolled her eyes. Then she began typing. "You are thoughtful of other folks' suffering."

"You see what good that did me. And them!" I reminded her.

"Doesn't matter. It's still a fine quality in a person." She drummed her keypad, pondered, then started typing again. "You are honest."

"I am not!"

"You 'fessed up about almost killing Ham, didn't you?" she asked. "And you told me about Baron. I could tell it was really hard for you, but you told it."

"But, still—"

She overrode me. "You are good at plants. You're smart."

"Now, come on!"

"You *try*. You don't give up on things." She tapped, *Doesn't give up.*

"Fine, good!" I can't explain it, but it was hard, hearing somebody say so many nice things about me. "Now what about you?"

"What about me?" Desiree asked.

"*Your* good things." I started counting things off on my fingers. "You're nice. And fun. And weird, but in a likeable way."

"Yeah?" She turned to look at me, her nose all crinkled with laughter.

"And you're beautiful," I added.

A curious moment passed right then, quiet and loud all at once.

Desiree took my hand. "Thank you, Hush. You're beautiful, too."

As for the list of amends, we decided to start with the most recent first: the imp stealing. That way, any ill that might yet come of the pain lifting could still be remedied.

Desiree and I sat looking at my jars of pain imps.

"I should offer to return them," I said. "But does it matter which one goes to who, do you think?"

She canted her head and considered. "Do they all look the same?"

I told her they did. "I reckon I can only try my best. All right. So let's begin with Mabel. It was her pain imp that started it all."

Desiree typed, *Mabel Holt—1 pain imp.*

It was hard to remember every person I'd plucked and how many imps they'd had, but in the end I think we got fairly close to the truth of it. And, boy howdy, did I have a big, long list of folks to make amends to.

"You know, they might not even believe me," I said. "Seeing as how I'll be carrying nothing but an empty-looking jar, offering nothing but the word of a known thief."

Desiree gave me a funny look. "Yeah, but, Hush, this is *Sass*."

"So?"

"Surely you know there's more magic in Sass than there are ankle biters at a lollipop stand?"

"Mabel did tell me about something called shines. And wish cakes."

"Yes! Exactly!" She straightened her glasses. "In Sass, people believe in magic. If you tell them you're a pain lifter—and remind them of how good they felt after you plucked their imps—they're going to believe you."

I goose-necked. "If you say so."

"Oh, *sure*!" That was Laura Lynn, one of my yoga students, getting all giddy. "Pain lifting! Sure! Old Nate Cunningham's granny used to have that shine!"

"I—I heard that, too." I was more than a little flummoxed by her response, even after Desiree's claims of magic and believers.

"So, you say you lifted some pain of mine?" Laura Lynn asked.

With a firm nod, I said, "Yes. Right there on your setter." I pointed to her right butt cheek.

She gave it a good think. "You know, it *has* been weeks since my hip last flared up! You did that?"

I hung my head. "I took it without your permission, yes, ma'am. But I want you to know, I think I can give it back, no harm done." Holding up my jar, I went on, "You'll have your pain just like it never left."

She scratched her chin with one long fingernail. "And, uh, why would I want that, exactly?"

"So you have your early-warning system. See, as I understand it, pain is a teacher, and it tells us we have to worry." I couldn't help feeling I didn't have that exactly right. "Point is, if something's wrong with you, but you don't have any pain, how will you know it? So if I give you back your pain, you'll know there's a problem."

Laura Lynn's laughter sounded like a rippling stream. "Oh, sugar! I know there's a problem! I've been crooked and slantwise since I was born! And unless I want to have surgery—which I do not—the only hope for me is your yoga class and, apparently, your pain lifting. So, if you're asking me to take my pain back, I think my answer is, thank you very kindly, but no!"

That left me somewhat addlepated, but after a moment's reflection, I remembered the cause for my going there: to make amends. If Laura Lynn didn't want her pain back, maybe I could still do right by her.

"You're surely within your rights. I wouldn't want unnecessary butt pain, neither," I said. "But I want to promise you: if you were to keep coming to my yoga class, I swear I would never lift another pain off you without asking first."

She thought that over. "That's very good of you."

I waited to see if she had any anger she wanted to ventilate, as the *Big Book* said she understandably might.

"That all?" she asked.

"That all with you?"

"Unless you want to buy a water purifier." It turned out Laura Lynn ran a small business out of her trunk.

"Not today. But thanks for offering."

That was pretty much how it went with most of the townsfolk. Nearly all of them believed I could—and did—lift their pain. And all but one said I was welcome to keep it, thank you very much.

"I reckon you should give back all of it," Ham said, his voice still a little raspy with the effort of healing. "Just to be on the safe side."

He was home from the hospital, but still under doctor's orders to rest, so I was sitting beside him in his bedroom, the TV on, but muted.

I unscrewed the jar lid and took out eight pain imps, the

number I'd plucked off of him over his weeks of yoga, plus the one from his appendix.

He looked at my cupped hand, but of course he couldn't see the imps. "Will it hurt?"

"I don't rightly know," I told him. "You're the first one who's wanted them back. They do give a little ache when I hold them in my hand."

He sighed. "All right. Let's have them."

I held one up after the other, each to the spot where I thought I remembered plucking it. Of the eight, only four took.

I tried again, and failed. "I'm sorry, Ham! Some of them won't stick."

"Which ones?"

I told him.

"Oh, well," he said. "The one on my arm was a burn from the grill. It's all healed up now. And my leg, that was just a pulled muscle. Those usually fix themselves fairly quick. The other two, whatever they were, must've cleared up, too."

I know it may seem silly, or even obvious to a smarter person, but I realized something right then: *I was not the only hope for removing folks' pain.* Sometimes suffering could heal on its own, without my help. Heck, I'd even seen hints of it before, when someone's pain imp winked out right before my eyes, but I hadn't really understood.

"What about the others? Do they hurt?" Of the four other imps that did stick, all but one looked fairly pale. That one, over his appendix, was darker.

"A little ache, like you said. Except for the incision. That one does smart." He shifted a little in his bed. "But I guess that's what the pills are for. I don't much like medicine," he confided.

I helped him get as comfortable as I could and even ran down to Beezer's to drop off that prescription he hadn't needed until he had his imps back. Before I left, I made him the same promise that I'd given to all my other imp-plucking victims: I would never again lift his pain without his say-so.

"That would probably be for the best," he sighed. "But it is a fine gift you have. I wouldn't set it on a shelf altogether."

"Maybe. Truth be told, it seems a lot bigger than one person can keep track of. I don't know how Granny Cunningham did it."

I was on my way out when I remembered something.

"Hey, Ham," I said. "Thanks for that day in the grocery store. Standing up to Nina."

"Happy to." His soft smile was a comfort to me. "How is your ma? I heard she had some trouble."

I looked down at my hands. "I, uh, I'm not sure." I hadn't seen her since that visit to the emergency room.

According to Desiree's database, Nina was the last, lone person on my imp-amends list.

NINA

Me and Mabel and Jimmy had a long talk about it—whether I should offer amends to Nina and, if so, how and when. It was hard because, even though I figured that I should make an apology, I couldn't help feeling that she owed me some amends, too. Underneath my worry for Nina's injuries, I was mad. I never deserved to be scourged with the lash of her heartlessness. But then again, if she'd been in so much pain that she couldn't think straight . . . I couldn't help recalling what she'd said in the emergency room about having a notion that she wasn't a real good ma.

The decision I finally came to—with Mabel and Jimmy's okay—was, no matter what Nina did or whether she ever volunteered her own amends, I did need to make an apology and offer her imps back.

Nina wasn't staying in 'Bagoville anymore, Jimmy told me. After the hospital, she'd decided to start fresh. So, she went to a place called Brandy's Family Lodge. It was "something like a halfway house, and something like a shelter, with people to help her heal and grow." I wasn't sure what to make of that, but it didn't really matter. That's where Nina was, and that's where I had to go.

The next morning, Mabel drove me and my imp jar to Brandy's.

Even though I'd never heard of it, the lodge was in town, not especially far from Desiree's house. It was a kind of square with a hole in the middle of it—four L-shaped apartments on the outside and a garden in the middle. Nina's apartment was number three.

"I'll wait here for you." Mabel eased herself backward onto a bench in the garden. So round and cumbersome, that baby was getting! "Call me if you need anything."

I told her I would. Then, after a fair amount of dilly-dallying, looking at the flowers and whatnot, I got up the nerve to knock on Nina's door.

All at once, there she was in the doorway. My ma. Her arm was still in a sling and her bruises had greened up something awful. Her pain imps hung on. But she did smile, and she even tried to hug me, which was mighty peculiar because neither of us really knew how to do it right.

The place was nice-ish inside, with a small brown sofa and carpets only a little stained. A book beside a lamp had the title *The Courage to Heal*. It was bookmarked at the halfway point. There was a table, too—that's where I set down the imp jar—and a couple chairs around it. I sat. After a pause, Nina took the seat next to me. We swapped nervous howdies.

Then there was a great deal of quiet.

All at once, a pressure built up in me—worse than a hundred locos and full of rage, on top of it.

The holler tore out of me. "How could you!"

Nina's eyes got big, but she didn't move, didn't speak.

"You were gonna send me off! To trick old people out of their money! You were going to grind out all the good left in me—which wasn't very much, thanks to you and your meanness! I'm your own flesh and blood, and you treated me like I was nothing! You called me names, you—you made fun of me for wanting toilet paper! You are a despisable good-for-nothing, and if there was an award for worst mother in the world, they wouldn't even consider you, because you're no mother at all!"

A pain imp over Nina's heart, already deep red, darkened to nearly black. Her good hand trembled as she seemed to search the tabletop for a thing she couldn't find.

"I came here to say sorry, and I reckon maybe I am!" I was surprised to find myself back on my feet, gripping the imp jar. "Not for you, but just for the fact that you're a human being who got hurt because of my gaum-up. Truth is, if there was any justice in this world, I'd dump this jar of pain imps over your head and you'd keep them all!"

Nina's eyes flicked toward the jar, which looked empty to her, of course.

"I ain't crazy!" I told her. "I'm just a little magical! You can't see them, but what's in this jar is pieces of pain. Yours plus other people's. I plucked some off of you before you told off Baron Ramey. That's why you felt so good. That's why you got beat up!"

Nina muttered something I couldn't hear.

"What?" I demanded in a half shout.

"I said I know you're not crazy," she replied. "I can see them, too."

A shock of white passed across my vision. "What?"

"I can see them. In the jar. On people. On you." She pointed a wobbly finger at my chest. "I just never knew what they was."

Maybe it was because I didn't want to be *anything* like Nina. Or it might have been knowing that we could have had something special to share, if only she'd been less harsh. But whatever it was, her words just froze me up.

"Excuse me." I headed for the door and slammed it behind me.

Outside, on her bench, Mabel scooted around so she could see me. Her expression of alarm told me just how strained I must have looked.

"Are you— Belle, what happened?"

"Nothing!" I threw my setter down on the bench. "That's not true. I didn't mean to lie. Something did happen."

She waited until I was ready to tell her.

"She can see them. The pain imps. She can see them, but she never knew what they were," I finally explained.

Mabel put an arm around my shoulders and gave me a squeeze.

"I hollered at her. A lot."

A wren landed at our feet and picked at a crumb.

"Can I do anything?" Mabel asked. "Did you want me to talk to her?"

I didn't answer her. Instead, I said, "I got to ask you something."

"Sure." Her arm was still around me.

Bracing myself for the worst, I asked, "What you said about me, to Jimmy and Ham and the sheriff. 'What did you expect?' What did you mean by that?"

I could see her trying to recall the moment. Her expression cleared and she explained, "I meant that we had pulled you out of your house, gave you no contact with your mother, surrounded you with strangers, and asked you to change your whole life in the blink of an eye. What did we expect? *Of course* you went to see Nina. *Of course* you wanted to make things right."

I thought about that, and I desperately wanted to believe her, but I had to be sure. "So, it weren't nothing about me being trailer trash and you expecting no better?"

"Oh, God! Belle! Is that what you thought?" Her eyes brimmed with water and her heart imp flared. "Never!

Never did I ever think such things about you! From day one, I have admired your strength and your good heart! If only *we* wouldn't fail *you*, I knew you'd do beautiful things with your life." She gave me a hard squeeze. "You already have."

I reckon I was getting better at hearing folks say nice things about me, because I didn't change the subject like I had at Desiree's. Instead, I leaned my head on her shoulder.

If there was an award for best pretend ma, Mabel would surely win top prize.

After a time, I told her, "It ain't finished. I still have to go back in."

I was a little more businesslike this time.

"So, what I got here, Nina, are the pain imps I stole while you were sleeping." I softly slapped the jar. "There were a lot of them, but you can have every one back, right here, right now. It's up to you. Either way, I vow to never pluck an imp from you, without your permission, again."

She nodded to let me know she understood.

"You just say the word," I told her.

She took the jar and gave it a little shake. The imps wobbled.

"Curious, how these little things made me so . . . well, made me what I was."

I confess, she did seem like a different person.

Even so, what she said surprised me. "I want to earn you

back, Hush. *Belle!* I know I don't deserve you. And it's crazy, because you're right. I've never been anything like a mother to you, so why would I want to start now? But something in me—like a heart urge, if that makes any sense—it says I *got* to try."

Her hands were fists as she said that.

"So, no, I don't think I *can* take those pain imps back. Because, with them on me, I'm— You're right, I'm despisable." She looked at me full-on. "I'd even ask you to pluck these ones off me—I can't see them, but you can—if not for the fact that I'm afraid to change *anything*! Afraid I'll go back to what I was!"

She dropped her chin to her chest and breathed a time or few.

"I accept your apology," she said once she'd picked up her head. "And I'd even like to make one of my own, except I know it'd be a drop in a big old sea. I reckon I'm going to have to spend the rest of my life making things up to you."

She had no right to the hope that might've flickered in my eyes, so I looked down at my shoes.

"I am *so* sorry!" Her voice cracked. "And I do *so* want you back. I know I can't make you come, though. Can't make you give me another chance. But I do want you to know, there's room for you here, and Brandy says we can stay as long as we need to. We'll never live in that motor home again! And, I swear, we'll always have toilet paper. Always!" She touched my arm ever so lightly. "Please at least think about it."

I moved so she couldn't reach my arm. Not out of spite, but because it hurt to feel her affection.

"Uh." I cleared my throat. "Thank you for, uh, for your offer. And your apology. I don't think I can give you an answer right now."

"Sure. Of course not," she said.

"I'll just take my jar and go."

"That's fine. Thanks for stopping by." She meant it. She was glad I'd come.

By the time I'd finished crying on Mabel's shoulder, her shirt was soaked through.

CRIMINAL

The next batch of amends was both easier and harder. Back when I'd got caught thieving at Dress Up, I'd made that whole list of all the things I ever stole. All I had to do was go ask JoBeth for it, and there was my list of wrongs right before me. Problem was, it was a fairly long list, years and years of borrowing. Even with my yoga earnings, I didn't have anywhere near the amount of money it would take to pay it all back.

I recalled Jimmy saying that a body could repay a debt by working it off. That sounded more hopeful to me. I mean, sure, there were only twenty-four hours in a day, and a person could only work off so much wrongdoing in that amount of time. But I was youngish, with lots of fit years ahead of me. Paying folks back with sweat equity, as Mabel might call it, seemed like a fairly good choice.

Desiree was right on top of things, typing my list of thievery into her little computer.

"See?" She pointed to her tablet. "When it's all laid out, it really isn't that much."

"Compared to who?" I laughed. "Jesse James? And I couldn't help noticing your own list of wrongdoings is a whopping three items long."

"Well, yeah," she agreed. "But they're dense! Really, really bad!"

"Like what? Read me one of them bad things you done."

She tapped the screen, flinging pages all around. "Here it is. Okay. I cheated on a test. See? Cheating is so *wrong*! Now you, in your case, a person could argue you might have been stealing to live. But nobody *has* to cheat. It's just wrong-wrong-wrong, no matter which way you cut it."

"Let me see that." I snatched up the tablet and read aloud, "'I accidentally looked up and saw that the teacher forgot to erase one of the answers from the board. I wrote the answer on my test sheet, even though I knew it was cheating.' Are you joshing me?"

"What? No!"

"Tell me something," I said, handing the tablet back.

"Okay."

"Did you know the right answer to the question, even without seeing it on the board?"

She looked off to the side. "Ye-ah."

I barked a laugh. "And this is the worst you got, huh?"

She blushed. "I *have* been very sheltered."

"Oh, Desiree. We have to dirty up them hands of yours! Just a little! Just so you can say you've lived!"

She leapt off her chair. "I would *love* that! Martin raises hell all the time, but I can't ever think of anything even remotely rascally!"

"I'll study on it," I promised. "See if we can't come up with something just a mite shady for you to do."

"Great! Could you just make sure it's after my chores are done?"

I figured it made the most sense to begin with the biggest borrow debt, then work my way down to the littler things. That meant starting with Beezer's.

"Miz Peggy," I began. "I need to talk to you about something."

We were standing on either side of the cash register while she counted the cash in her drawer. Considering my past, that there's what you call trust.

"Yeah? *Fifteen, sixteen, seventeen—*"

"I'll wait till you're done."

She finished up the counting and closed the drawer. "What is it, sugar?"

I filled my lungs and spilled it out. "I am embarrassed to call your attention to it, but the truth is, over the years, I have stolen a great many things from your store. I would like to make amends for all that thieving by paying you back in sweat equity."

Then I had to explain what *sweat equity* meant.

"Oh, Hush." She shook her head. "Please, don't worry about it. I know you've been working hard to turn over a new leaf. Let's call it water under the bridge. I mean, how much could you possibly owe me?"

Thanks to Desiree's database, I had the number handy. "One thousand seven hundred sixty-two dollars. Give or take."

Her jaw dropped.

"As—as I said, I'd be glad to work off the debt! I have to give Mabel Holt four hours a day, then my yoga classes, but that leaves a couple hours every day before you close." I glanced around. "There's got to be tons of things that need doing! Those shelves are awful dusty, for instance. And that soap display, so close to the door the way it is, you're practically asking for folks to steal from you."

She was still collecting herself, but she did manage to say, "I am, am I?"

"Yes, ma'am. Actually, there's a heap of things I could tell you about thief-proofing this place." I pointed to the Fine Gifts case. "I mean, you can't tell me those earbobs ain't been walking out of here right and left. And it's not me, I swear! I only took the one set."

She walked over to the earbobs and gave them a quick count. "I do seem to be missing a few pair. And those kids from Dietz *were* in here twice last week. . . ."

"See what I mean?" I asked.

"I think I do," Peggy replied. "Hush, I think I would like to have you work off some of your debt."

I let out a *whoosh* of relief. "Thank you. Making up for this stuff really does lift a weight off a person. So, where do you want me to start? Dusting those shelves?"

"No, nothing like that." She walked away and came back with two folding chairs. "Sit down, sugar. I'm hiring you as my anti-theft consultant."

After only a week of work, Peggy felt I'd more than repaid her, considering the money she'd save with her new thief-foiling strategies. Word got around, too, and three other stores I'd stolen from wanted me to consult for them. It wasn't long before the whole Sass retail district was locked down tighter than your skinny sister's underpants.

The amends list was emptying out very nicely, and I was getting down to the petty steals, the things I took from lone people instead of stores. Lots of these things were pickpockety stuff, small, but probably more meaningful to a person than a can of tuna was to Mister Hopps down at Sass Foods.

I was thinking of one particular item, a broken watch I once pinched from a man's pocket. It was the round kind with a chain, and inside it, it said "From one old dingo to another, yuk-yuk-yuk!" Now, I hadn't known who the man was then, but having spent more time in town, getting to know folks, I was fairly sure the old dingo was named Mister Barker. And from the silliness of the engraved words, I had a good feeling that Mister Barker would prefer to have the watch back, instead of some cold lump of dollars, or me mowing his lawn for a month.

Problem was, the watch—along with a number of other things like it—was back in 'Bagoville, in one of my stashes.

But *was* it a problem? After all, it wasn't like Nina was staying at the RV anymore, so I wasn't prohibited from going on that account. And it was my own house. Besides, I was supposed to be able to go where I pleased, as long as I didn't do it alone. Now that I thought on it, there was no good reason why I shouldn't go clear out my stashes and return every single borrow to its proper owner. Plus—and I couldn't help smiling at the notion—here was a great chance to give Desiree her little sashay on the wild side. I could teach her how to pick the RV lock! And since it was *my* motor home, and I was giving her permission, she wouldn't have really done anything wrong at all.

I planned the 'Bagoville run for early the next morning, so it didn't conflict with Desiree's chores or one of my umpteen jobs. I meant to tell Mabel and Jimmy all about it that night, even down to the bit of lock-picking tomfoolery, but we got caught up in some sober talk about Nina's new place and what might happen when the summer was over. Things turned so serious and upsetting, I forgot to mention my stash grab.

That morning, the sunlight shone nearly white, so the world even *looked* hot.

Desiree and I ate breakfast on the porch while Mabel fiddled with a new recipe she was thinking of serving for Travis and Tom's homecoming. I tried not to cogitate much on that, as it meant the end of summer was coming up fast.

"If I lived at Brandy's Lodge," I asked Desiree, "would you visit me?"

Mouth full of raisin toast, she nodded her reply. She swallowed and added, "And it's on my way to school. We could walk together."

For the first time, it struck me. School! With a whole town's eyes upon me, there'd be no way to shirk my education now!

"I reckon we could," I agreed. "But I don't think I'd be in your class, having missed two years and all." The notion of sitting in a room filled with younger kids pinked me up with shame.

"Hmm," Desiree mused. "We've got a little while before school starts. I wonder if I could help you catch up."

I couldn't help feeling that wasn't too likely.

Though I had no particular need of it, I left Mabel's place with my imp jar under my arm. I guess I'd become accustomed to having it with me. Desiree chatter-peeped like a happy bird as we walked, all aflutter about her upcoming "hoodlumism," as she was calling it.

"Martin will be so jealous! He can't pick a lock!"

I couldn't help admiring the glint of sweet mischief in her eye.

"I know because I found him swearing at Dad's file cabinet, trying to jam his driver's license into one of the drawer gaps."

"What was he looking for?" I asked.

"His music. Dad confiscates it when Martin's on restriction."

We rounded a corner and turned onto the dirt road that ran by 'Bagoville. In the glaring sun—especially now that I'd become accustomed to the niceties of town—even the trees looked tired and poor.

"You reckon you really want to see this?" I asked before we got too close.

"I've seen 'Bagoville before, Hush!"

"Yeah, but you ain't seen it knowing I lived there."

She stepped in front of me, walking backward, and poked my shoulder with each word: "I. Like. You. No. Matter. What!"

"All right," I chuckled. "I hear ya."

With Nina gone, the old place looked more forlorn than ever. A full-on mosquito farm was growing in the puddle that had collected in Nina's ash can. The black-water stench carried a fair piece farther.

Things were too quiet.

All at once, I wanted to quick-finish the job and get us back to Mabel's.

"All right, Mizzy Lockpick Lady, let's get it done!" I took Desiree by the shoulders and set her before the door lock.

It didn't take long. The flash of an unbent paper clip, the wiggle of a tumbler, and we were in.

"I did it!" Desiree spun around and grabbed me. "I feel so *bad*! In a good way!"

I enjoyed her smile for the breadth of a gnat's hair, then flung open the door and led her inside.

"I won't be but a minute." I set down the imp jar and dumped out a box of junk.

While I was busy refilling the box from one stash, then another, Desiree made her way back to the bed and bounced on it a time or two.

"It's kinda cozy," she remarked.

"Cozy, if you got nowhere else to go," I told her.

"Mmm." She seemed to agree. "So, how many stashes do you have?"

"Five in here," I replied. "There's one outside, too, but I reckon it's wet and stank." It was in a compartment just behind the black-water shaft, where I'd known nobody would mess with it. I reckoned I'd been right. Even *I* didn't want to go there. "Two more to go."

I popped the panel off the radio hole and came out with the Orrs' floss, then my treasure map. Half grinning, I set both of them in the box.

"Hey, Desiree?"

"Yeah?"

"You remember the first time I was at your house and Martin called me Smell Cantrell?"

"Yeah."

"Do you think—"

A terrible creak sounded. It was the sound of a door being opened—not by a breeze, but by an unwelcome hand. Even without looking, I knew who it was. I knew it with every shred of my intuition.

To Desiree, I mouthed, *It's Baron!*

I saw her breath freeze in her chest.

There isn't much free space inside a motor home. You've got one row of carpet where you can travel forward, to the driver's seat, or backward, toward the bed.

I leapt from my spot between the front seats, hoping against hope that I could get to a kitchen drawer to grab something, *anything* I could defend us with. As my body fairly flew through the air, Baron Ramey's long-fingered hand shot in through the door and caught me square on the chest.

Baron shouldered into the already cramped space and took a look around. He had but one pain imp on him, a cruel black-red one. Only the very tippy-tail of it twitched between his eyebrows—as if it had burrowed into his brain.

"Well, well," he drawled, closing a fist around the fabric of my shirt. "The prodigal child returneth." Pulling me toward him so hard I stumbled, he leered. "How the heck are you, girl?"

I was snarling my reply when I heard a "Yeeeeeee-aaaaaaahhh!" tear through the musty air. Desiree's plan, as far as I could guess, was to launch herself from the bed and throw her leg into the space between me and Baron, making a good try for his family jewels. Quarters were tight, though, and she caught her side on the sharp edge of the kitchen counter. She yelped with the pain of it and crumpled to the floor.

"Well, well," he said again. "Two for the price of one!"

"You're disgusting." I spat in his face.

The muscles of his jaw turned hard. "I was ready to be buddies. But that there warrants some punishment." He pulled me so close I could smell his rotten breath. "Here's what's going to save you, if you're smart. Nina was supposed to meet me today. And she didn't. You are going to tell me where she is. Right now."

Desiree picked up her head. Voice steady as all get-out, she told Ramey, "You let her go."

Baron ignored her. "I'll find your ma, Hush. You know I will. But if you make it too hard for me, I'll be mad when I find her. I might lose control. You know what that could look like."

I thought of Nina laying in the hospital, pain imps blazing. It could be worse, I knew. It could be ten *times* worse.

"Save her"—he shook me once—"and you—a world of hurt. *Where is she?*"

I knew one thing for certain: If he found Nina, she was done for. Baron could talk about going easy on her, but I knew different. He'd have his revenge for her willfulness, and that was that.

What I really needed was a way to keep Desiree and me safe, and get us both to the police department so I could warn the sheriff about Baron's plans for Nina.

Desiree started to push herself up to her knees.

"Stay down, little girl," Baron drawled at her.

I railed at my own foolishness. What was I thinking, bringing Desiree to 'Bagoville? I just *had* to have my stash! Had to dazzle her with the picking of a stupid, half-broke lock!

Right then, I decided I would not—would not *ever*—let another person be hurt because of my mistake. *Especially* not my special, crazy friend.

I cast Desiree a look that I hoped said, *Follow my lead.* Then I told Baron, "Nina's new address is outside. In my back stash. Desiree knows where it is."

"Is that so, *Desiree?*" I hated the way he held her name in his mouth.

"Yes," she lied bravely.

"Go get it, then," snarled Baron.

"I got to help her—" I said.

"Bull." He choked up on my shirt. "Go get the address, girl. Me and Hush'll wait here."

Desiree glanced at me as she scrambled up. There weren't nothing in her eyes but unwavering trust and love.

Only love is real. That's what Crispy had said.

And a dying man ought to know.

From Crispy's lips to your ear, BP! I prayed.

While Baron shifted sideways to let Desiree pass, I quick set my eyes on the imp jar, just a few feet away.

"Don't you think about running off, girl!" Baron shouted at Desiree as she stepped outside.

All at once, I felt bushels stronger. *She's out! She's safe! Oh, Desiree! Please run!*

No matter how scared my friend was, though, I knew she'd never leave me alone with Baron.

"I've got it!" Desiree called, spinning a fable. "It says, fourteen-thirty . . . something. Or fifty something? Seabass Singer Street? Does that sound right? Hush, I can't make out your writing."

"It's Nina's writing. I can't never make it out, neither." My reply was a fib, but my voice was shaking for real.

"Aw, heck. Bring the paper here." Baron let go of my shirt and shoved me backward, hard.

The refrigerator handle bruised my back, but I didn't care. Baron was balanced in the RV doorway, half in, half out, distracted. In a flash, I grabbed the imp jar and un-screwed the lid.

"Where are you, girl?" he called to Desiree.

"I'm over here!"

I could tell she was shouting from back behind the RV. If only I could keep Ramey from reaching her!

Please, please, please—

I stepped to the door, tapped Baron on the shoulder, and when he turned his face toward me—I flung the whole jar's worth of pain imps right at him.

And then, with a special, extra brain-shove, I added, *Stick!*

A howl tore through the white-hot air of 'Bagoville. A hundred imps or more latched onto Baron Ramey, every one of them flaring deep red. He fell down the steps, landing on the ground with a grunt.

I launched myself out of the motor home, found Desiree, and pulled her to my cousin's RV. Banging on the door, I shouted, "Sheena! I know you're in there! Call the police! Call them now!"

Meantime, Baron rolled all around, swearing, clutching his face as if he'd been pepper-sprayed.

I got hold of Desiree and meant to hide us in a junk car, but we were only halfway there when I heard sirens wail. Creation, was I glad for the bittiness of Podunk Sass! The sheriff must've already been in the neighborhood!

It turned out it wasn't Sheena who'd called the police, but a code-enforcement lady who'd heard Baron's scream. I wasn't too happy with Cousin Sheena after that, so the couple of things I still had that I'd borrowed from her, I set out on her front step with a note that said, "Sorry. But not *too* sorry."

There was a fair bunch of busy-ness after Sheriff Thrasher arrived. Since it didn't seem fitting to drive Baron to the jail with me and Desiree sitting in the front seat, the police had to ask the PD in Pitney if they'd lend a hand. Sass had only one police car. As I said, *Po-dunk.* I did ask if JoBeth might carry Desiree and me to the station on the back of the department's ATV, but the sheriff wouldn't allow it.

As the two of us sat on a pile of tires, waiting for our ride, I asked Desiree, "You all right?"

"Yes," she said. Then, with a nervous smile, "No. I think I peed myself. I was so scared."

Truth was, I'd been scared, too. But more than that, I'd been *mad*. And it was the mad, somehow, that got me through. I'd heard folks say a body can't think clearly when they're riled, and that may be true for some. But just for me, on that particular morning, my ire had given me the courage to stand up to Baron.

Of course, it wasn't *just* the anger.

"Yeah, it was fearsome," I said. "But somewhere inside me, I knew: *Me and Desiree didn't meet just so we could get thrashed by some cur.* There was something Bigger at work. Something on our side. Otherwise, why would those imps have stuck?"

231

Desiree dipped her head to the side. "It *could* have been some new part of your magic that you didn't know about."

I was about to say something counter to that when she added, "But . . . maybe it's six of one, half dozen of the other. Surely your magic comes from something Bigger. I mean, where else could it possibly come from?"

The police car scooped us up and dropped us off at what was fast becoming my new home away from home—the hospital. Yup. Three times in three weeks, though this was my first visit as a patient.

Me and Desiree refused to let them split us up, so we sat atop the same emergency-room table while a doctor peered into our eyes and asked us about a hundred questions. We were telling her no, neither of us did feel dizzy, when I heard a voice scream out, "Call Tom and Travis! Oh! Ow! Hasn't *anyone* seen Belle?"

I knew the voice with a certainty. And even before I peeked out through the curtain and saw Nurse Cussler rolling Mabel down the hall in a wheelchair, I knew another thing, too: Mabel was having her baby. Early.

BEGINNING

"Gotta go!" I shouted to Desiree, skidding into the hall. "Wait up! Mabel! It's Belle!"

"Hold up! Hold up!" Mabel yelled at the nurse.

Mabel reached out and nearly hugged me to pieces. "Oh, Belle, thank— Ow! Ow! Ow!" Eyes squeezed shut against the pain, she made a circling motion with her finger. "Rolling. Let's roll, please." She had more imps around her middle than I could count at a glance.

Mabel, Nurse Cussler, and me flew at the speed of wheelchair down one hallway and up another. We swerved into a quiet little room, set apart from the others, decorated in soft baby-type hues. There was every manner of alarming beepmachines, plus a table full of wicked-looking metal devices, but there was also a tiny crib and a right comfortable-looking set of chairs, each draped with a blanket.

"Nurse," I said, gluing myself to Mabel's side. "Can you tell us if it's very dire, the baby coming so early?"

She put a plastic clip on Mabel's fingertip. "It's not what we hoped for. But Mabel is healthy. And I bet your yoga class was a big help, too."

It was fine praise that didn't matter to me one whit. "But you'll help her all you can, right?"

Nurse Cussler was forming her answer when a man rushed in. From his white coat and fancy shoes, I figured he must be the doctor.

"Came as soon as I got your call, Mabel," he said. "How are you?"

"I'm in labor, Zeke! How do you think I am?"

It was the first—and only—time I ever heard Mabel get snarky. I might have smiled, except I knew it was the pain getting to her.

"'Cut the small talk, Doc.' Understood," Zeke said, smiling. "Lainey, what with the baby being early, I think I'd like to use one of the surgical rooms."

The nurse nodded. "I'll make sure we're all set in there." Turning my way, she asked, "Can you stay with her?"

"Of course!"

With the doctor and nurse gone, I dropped to my knees at the foot of Mabel's chair. "What can I do?"

She grabbed my hand. "I am so glad you're here. Um." Her eyes went out of focus and she cried out. When she came back to me, she said, "Can you make sure they called Tom and Travis? The number's in my purse. In the thingy, here." She tried to point toward the pocket on the back of the wheelchair.

"I see it. You just reeeelax. Maybe do some of that yoga breathing." I grabbed her bag, fished out the number, and dialed it on the house phone.

A sliver of a ring sounded, then: "Hello! Mabs?"

"Tom! This is Belle!" Thankfully, he knew me from our small talk while Mabel had been a-waddling to the phone these last few weeks. "Mabel wanted me to call you—"

"Tell her we're on our way! We're on our way!"

"How long do you think—?"

"Hold on—jeez! Atlanta drivers! Sorry, Belle! The traffic's really bad. Two hours. At least. Tell her—ugh! Belle, I gotta go. Tell her we'll be there as soon as we can!"

Another voice came on the line. "Hey, Belle. It's Travis. Give her a peck for me. Tell her I know she can do it."

"Don't you talk like that!" I heard Tom in the background. "We are going to get there on time to see that baby being— OH, COME ON!"

"See you soon," Travis said, and hung up.

Mabel looked up hopefully. "Well?"

"They're coming. As fast as they safely can."

"How long?"

I told her.

She shook her head hard and fast—partly a denial, I thought, and partly a new contraction. "They're gonna miss it." A new pain imp appeared over her heart.

I couldn't make the men appear any faster, but there was one thing I could do.

I knelt down again. "You got about fifty little red guys wiggling around your midsection. Can I help you some?"

"Pain imps, you mean?" Her eyes went distant again.

When they cleared up, I said, "Yeah. Pain imps. Want me to pluck a few?"

She didn't even think it over. "No. Thanks. I need— I *want* to feel this."

I tell you, it was the hardest thing I ever did, keeping my hands off those imps while they flared red and redder yet, till they weren't nothing but a wild and constant crimson.

"Hold my hands," Mabel pleaded.

I did.

"Can I squeeze?" she asked. "It'll hurt."

"You can break my fingers if you have to." I grinned. "We're in a hospital. They can fix me right up."

She smiled weakly. "Thank you, honey." Then she squeezed. Not so weakly.

"Ye gods, woman! You're strong!" But I loved that pain in my hands, because I knew it meant Mabel would have strength enough to deliver her baby safe and sound.

The nurse rushed back in, flipped the brake off the wheelchair, and started rolling Mabel away before I could even get to my feet.

"Belle!" Mabel called.

I raced after them. "I can come, right?"

The doctor must have heard me, because he shouted from behind a pair of doors, "No minors in the delivery room!"

"Rule toady!" I shouted back. Hoping the nurse would be more reasonable, I whisper-pleaded, "Let me sneak in once his back's turned!"

She shook her head. "Can't. But she'll be out soon."

"Real soon!" Mabel moaned.

The chair kept on rolling.

"Mabel! Travis sends a kiss! He says he knows you can do it!"

"Thank you!" As she disappeared behind the swinging doors, she called out, "I love you, Belle!"

I pressed my face to the crack between the doors and hollered, "I love you, too!"

It was the first time I ever said those words.

Shaw Reilly Holt was born at 12:37 in the afternoon. He was healthy, pink, and—dog my cats!—that little guy could wail!

They set Mabel up in that baby-colored room, with little Shaw in the crib. And this time, there was *no* getting rid of me. I was glued to Mabel's side, even while she nursed the baby, even while she drowsed. Right up until the second that Tom and Travis appeared in the doorway, so many balloons floating around their heads that it was hard to make out their faces.

All manner of hugs and kisses followed, and, of course, none of that involved me. Why should it? I wasn't one of the family, after all. Still, I couldn't say it didn't hurt some, standing in the far back of that room, witnessing a sort of gladness I'd surely never know. Though I couldn't see it—there was no mirror in the room—I was fairly certain I felt a pain imp being born from my heart.

While they were all smitten with Shaw, cooing over him and feeling his tiny hand grasp their fingers, it seemed like a good time to slip out. I wasn't sure what to do or where to go. Clearly all the bedrooms in Mabel's house would be taken up, with the baby here and the menfolk home. I wasn't ready to go to Nina's, though. If I ever would be. I wondered if I could stay at the hospital. There was a food machine at the end of the hall, and a chair where I could sleep. They might allow it if I went back down to the ER and told them, yeah, I *was* a little dizzy after that ruckus with Baron Ramey. Well, not dizzy, precisely. Maybe just done in.

I was feeling in my pocket for snack change—and feeling my loco a little, reminding me there was a gift cart in the lobby of the hospital—when I saw a yellow-headed figure sitting by the vending machines.

I called out, "You been waiting here this whole time?"

Desiree twisted around in her seat. "Hush! How are they?"

"They're good," I told her. "Baby's early but fine. Mabel's tired, but that's only fitting. She's happy."

"I'm *so* glad. And you? How are you?" she wanted to know.

I felt my grin falter. "Why would I be anything other than peart?"

She walked up. Taking hold of my hand, she poured me a dozen or so peanuts from a cellophane package. "Because it's over."

I closed my fist around the nuts. "What's over?"

"Your new beginning," Desiree replied. "Mabel's house is filling up again. School's starting soon. Things are going to change."

How can you see my troubles so clear? I nearly asked. But of course she *would* see. She saw everything.

"You're right. It's the end. I'll own . . . it does hurt." Head hung low, I set my back against one of them bright-white hospital walls.

"Hush Cantrell, you don't listen so good." She tugged on my sleeve. "I didn't say it was the end. I said it was the end of the beginning."

I chewed on that. "Not sure what you're getting at."

A voice from a speaker called Nurse Cussler to the front desk. After its echo died out, Desiree said, "In the *beginning* of something, we're tiptoeing. Figuring stuff out. Things are interesting—but they're scary."

She folded up her peanut package and slipped it in her pocket. "In the *middle*, though, we steady up. We know what's what. We don't have to think so much about, oh, just squeaking by. We can start to have fun."

"Aw, you can't tell me this morning wasn't fun," I teased. Maybe it was a poor joke. Surely Baron Ramey was no laughing matter.

But she only smiled. "Different fun. Better fun. The kind of fun that can become something . . . real." She thought for a second. "It took me a long time to learn to see the horse witches. But now I see them, and other things, too. Things wild and strange—and magical. I see the dance of nature."

With a sudden *swoosh*, she threw open her arms. "Welcome to the beginning of the middle!"

I looked at her good and close. All at once, the blue light of her eyes shone with a fresh magic. It was something like *believing*, if you can make any sense of that. And it made me want to believe, too. Believe in *what*, I wasn't quite sure. Maybe in *us*, twelve years old and breathing strong. Maybe in something without a name.

We finished up Desiree's peanuts, then ate a whole 'nother package.

My growling stomach had me contemplating a third, when Desiree asked, "Think we could go in and look at the baby?"

A goodly amount of time had passed, I reasoned, so maybe we wouldn't be a bother to the Holts. I had to think of them that way. The Holts. It wasn't just Mabel anymore.

"Let's go see," I replied.

———

From the doorway, I checked to be sure it wasn't some greeting-card moment we were about to bust in on.

Tom had pushed one of those comfy chairs up to the bed. He was sprawled out, fast asleep. Mabel was gazing dreamily out the window, her arm reaching out to play with Tom's hair. Closer to us, Travis and a freckly girl—the one from the pictures on his closet—stood over Shaw's crib.

Travis spoke real low, but I heard him say to the girl, "Do you ever think . . . someday, you and me—?"

"Travis Tromp!" The girl spun, her hand poised in front of Travis's forehead, fixin' to flick. "If you utter one more syllable, I swear I will thump you before Shaw and everyone!"

"Dang, Genuine. I said *someday*."

But they were both smiling, and I knew the whole thing was a playfulness between them.

Mabel looked up about that time and saw me and Desiree standing in the door.

"Hey!" she whispered. "Come in!"

Travis and his friend stepped back so Desiree could get a gander of Shaw's sweet face. Me, I sat on the edge of Mabel's bed. I was glad to see most of her pain imps were a pale red. A few had even disappeared entirely.

"Where'd you run off to?" she asked.

I shrugged. "You had other company."

She gave Tom's head a pat. "I know you don't know these guys yet, but they're great. You'll like them."

It was hard to know what to say to that. "I reckon they're very fine."

"They'll be going back to the house tonight," Mabel went on. "But I'll be staying here till morning."

"Sure. You need to rest."

"That chair folds out to a single bed." She pointed to one of the soft seats. "I was hoping you might stay with me."

It wasn't pity that made her ask it. I could see it, plain as day. *She wanted me there.* Even with the baby born and Travis and Tom back, she still wanted me there.

"Tomorrow," she mused, "you could come back to the house. Tom's a fair cook, but I could really use a skilled hand in the garden until the end of the season."

It was a nice notion, but . . . "There won't be any room, with Tom and Travis in the house, plus the baby."

She waved away the problem. "Tom is staying, but Travis is heading to some RNN meeting with his dad. You won't even have to move your stuff." She poked my leg. "I really would love to have you there. And it would give you some time to think things over."

"You mean about where I'm headed after summer," I said.

"Yeah, that. But other things, too."

That fold-out hospital chair was so downright comfortable that I toyed with the idea of how a person might go about sneak thieving such a thing. Could I put a sheet over it and roll it out, like a wheelchair? Pretend I was a charity volunteer come to pick it up for donation? And once I got the thing out, where would I put it? In the middle of my cell at juvie?

They were just silly thoughts, of course, a way of keeping my mind off the bigger things. I sure as heck wasn't sleeping.

The next morning, after Mabel fed the baby, I told her about 'Bagoville and Baron Ramey. What with the baby squeezings and all, she hadn't heard.

She gripped a pillow as I spoke, her expression tight with worry. "But they've got him now, right? It's over?"

"Mostly," I told her. "The sheriff said he wanted to talk to me and Desiree, with you and Jimmy there. I reckon Jimmy will be enough, though, since you're laid up."

Mabel shook her head. "The sheriff can come to my house. I'm not leaving you to do that on your own."

"Oh, I won't be alone—"

"Belle." She dropped her chin all serious-like. "I'll be there."

It was a big hooray, getting Mabel and Shaw out of the hospital and back home. And when we finally got there, so many folks had stopped by with balloons and stuffed bears and flowers, it was another huge to-do just clearing a path to get mama and son into the house.

Eventually, though, we got everyone settled. Travis left shortly after, and the four of us—Tom, Mabel, Shaw, and me—crawled into our respective beds and slept until the baby's hungry cries woke us some hours later.

The next morning, Sheriff Thrasher came by, along with Desiree and Jimmy. After a heap of questions, he thanked us for our help and was fixin' to leave.

"Hold up, Hush. I want to show you something in my car."

The sheriff led me out to his cruiser and lifted out my box of borrows, the one I'd filled from my stashes the day before.

"I found this while I was going over the scene." The sheriff fixed me with a knowing eye. "There's some funny stuff in here that don't seem like it's yours. . . ."

"No, sir," I agreed. "Most of that's things I stole. That's why Desiree and me went to 'Bagoville in the first place. I was planning to collect those things and return them to their owners."

After a look that could have out-detected a lie detector, he said, "See that you do."

He was getting into the car when I stopped him. "Sheriff?"

"Yes, Hush?"

"He is going to jail, right? Baron Ramey?" I confess, just saying that name out loud gave me a nervous jolt.

He gave a sharp cop's nod. "Threatening young girls? *And* your mama willing to press charges? I expect the judge will put him away for a long time."

GIFT

That night, while Shaw slept, us big folks sat down to Tom's triple-decker club sandwiches. I was three bites into mine when someone knocked at the door.

"Y'all stay put," I said. "I'll get it."

I was wiping my cheek with my napkin as I opened the door.

Standing on the porch—and holding a stuffed bunny— was Nina.

My heart dropped into my gut.

"Can I come in?" she asked.

"Uh, I don't—"

I felt, rather than saw, Mabel appear behind me.

"Nina! Of course you can come in. We were just sitting down to dinner." In a louder voice, she called, "Tom, would you make up another club?"

"I don't know if I'm supposed to be here," Nina admitted,

stepping into the house. "But I heard the baby came early." She offered the bunny to Mabel.

It took me a second to realize the rabbit was a gift for Shaw. *My mother had brought a present to Mabel's boy!*

It was a gladness and a sorrow, both. Baby Shaw deserved all the good things the world could bestow on him. But hadn't *I* once hoped and longed for a toy not so different from that bunny?

Mabel accepted the stuffed critter. "Thank you, Nina. That's very kind."

"I also heard about"—Nina swallowed—"Baron. I wanted to make sure everyone was all right." Her eyes darted back from Mabel to me. *"Are* you all right?"

I nodded.

She threw herself on me and hugged so hard I couldn't take a breath. "I'm so, so sorry! It was all my fault! I know it was!"

"I know it was, too," I said, pulling away.

Mabel jerked her chin back. There wasn't any fault-finding in her expression, precisely, but the Mabel in my head said, *You can do better than that.*

Maybe I don't want *to do better*, I thought. But it was only a passing thing. The spite in me wasn't so strong anymore.

"But not *only* your fault," I admitted to Nina. "I reckon you never told Baron to bully my friend."

Her hand fluttered up to her heart, passing ghostlike through the deep red imps on her chest. "Is your friend all right?"

Nina won herself some points there, asking about Desiree.

"Yeah. She's okay." I sighed and added, "*Did* you want to come in for some food?"

"I don't want to be any trouble."

"It's fine, Nina," Mabel told her. "Come in. We should probably have a sit-down, anyway."

We sat down. Tom brought a fresh sandwich for Nina and excused himself to check on Shaw.

Nina and Mabel traded uneasy smiles.

"I'm staying here the rest of the summer!" was how I started things off. Loudly.

"Oh," Nina said. "Uh. That's, uh, that's all right with you, Miz Holt?"

"Call me Mabel. Yes. I'm glad to have her."

"Well. Good, then."

Somewhere nearby, a clock ticked.

Tick.

Tick.

Nina looked down at her plate. "This is a mighty big sandwich."

Mabel laughed. "Tom was a bachelor for a lot of years—"

"If I come live with you," I blurted, "we're gonna need some ground rules! Big-time!"

"Uh, sure. Ground rules," Nina stammered. "I agree."

"Number one!" I held up a finger. "No con artists, no shady guests. If you have cause for legitimate company, you can meet them in the garden." I mulled that over. "Or at Ham's, if it's raining. Can you live with that?" I spoke it like a challenge, which, truth to tell, it was.

Then Nina did something that left me slack-jawed. She asked Mabel for pen and paper. When Mabel brought them, Nina picked up the pen and wrote, *ONLY LEGITIMATE COMPANY. IN GARDEN OR AT HAM'S.*

"What else?" my mother asked.

When I found my voice, I said, "No drinking. No smoking. Well, no. Smoking only in the garden until you can quit. You have an addiction, and fixing that can take time. I got a book you can read."

Nina wrote, *NO DRINKING. SMOKING—GARDEN— QUIT. READ BOOK.*

I went on, "Even if you ain't quit yet, if we're low on money, we always buy toilet paper and food before cigarettes."

She took all that down. "Go on."

The next one was harder, mostly because it had a big, fat ribbon of shame tied around it. "There will be no poking fun in our house. Ever. You belittle me even one time, laugh at me, call me a nasty name—*anything*—and I swear, woman, you will *never* see me again."

Nina set down the pen and put her face in her hands. Two of her heart imps went crimson. It was a while before she said, "I was a fool to think—how *could* you ever forgive me? I've broken everything!"

Mabel and I swapped glances.

248

What do I do? I asked with a bite of my lip.

Mabel canted her head. *What do you* want *to do?* I imagined her saying.

One rageful chunk of me still wanted to throw nasty words at Nina and treat her like a dog. To hurt her as bad as she'd hurt me.

A lot of me, though, couldn't help recalling the way she'd whimpered in her sleep that one night in our RV, about a hundred years ago. A line from the *Big Book* came to me, too: *People who hurt, hurt people.*

Dang it.

I closed my eyes and sent up a wish—a true, deep wish—for a heart that could love through the pain.

"Nina," I finally said. "You didn't break everything. You didn't break me. And *that* is how, someday, I'm gonna be able to forgive you."

. . .

Not long after, we got word that Crispy had died. Mabel, who'd known him well, was sad, of course. But me, I couldn't help recalling how much he'd looked forward to seeing his mama and his wife again. I remembered the handmade poster in his room, GRANPA'S BIG ADVENCHER! More than anything, I was glad for him.

His memorial service was simple and small, just a handful of people in the chapel of the Pitney hospice. Roxie

Fuller was there, wearing purple. When I admitted to her how excited I was for Crispy's new beginning, she smiled and whispered, "Me too!"

A couple weeks after that, a letter came to Mabel's house, addressed to me. It was from a lawyer. Unopened envelope in hand, I plunked down on the floor to fret. I'd returned all my borrowed items to their owners, and nearly every one of them had accepted my apologies. Mister Barker even bought me an ice cream cone; that's how glad he was to see his watch again. But maybe someone had a change of heart. Maybe they were pressing charges.

"Maybe you should just open it," Mabel suggested, hefting Shaw from one shoulder to the other.

She was right. If "just desserts" were coming my way, best to take out my spoon and start chomping.

Good day, Miss Cantrell, the letter began. *I am writing on behalf of the estate of Mr. Dalton "Crispy" Freye. You have been named as a beneficiary in his will. It was his desire that these items from his estate be given to you. Item one—*

At first, I couldn't even make sense of it. I had to read the letter five times before it sunk in.

"What's it say?" Mabel finally asked.

"It says . . ." I shook my head in disbelief. "It says I got a cow! Of my very own! And a stall to keep her in! With pasture she can graze for free! At a place called Crispy Acres."

"That's a beautiful place for a cow," Mabel observed. "Very peaceful."

Dropping my hands into my lap, I wondered, "Why would Crispy leave me a cow? You and Becky Orr are the only people who even know I like cows." Of course, it didn't take me long to connect those dots. "*You* told him?"

Mabel reached for a rag and set it under the baby's drool-sopped chin. "He had a nurse call me to ask if there was anything you needed or wanted. I was just joking, but I said you might like a cow."

My cockles warmed at the idea that Mabel cared enough about me to recall one tiny piece of one tiny talk we'd had so long ago.

"I still don't understand why would he do it in the first place," I said.

"You eased his heart in his last days, helping him resolve things with Roxie," she said. "He was grateful."

In the eye of my mind, I saw Crispy's relief after I'd promised to deliver his apology. I recalled, too, how the amends I'd made had lightened my own heart's burden.

Holding up the letter, I protested, "But *this*? It's too much!"

Mabel gave a half shrug. "Maybe. But it was his to give."

REAL

Those last two weeks of summer, I was living all over the map. Most nights I spent at Mabel's, but a couple times I stayed with Nina at Brandy's Lodge, just to see how it felt. Daytimes, when I wasn't working in Mabel's garden or teaching yoga, I got to know my new cow. It turned out she carried a calf! I decided to name her Bitsy—Bit for short—in anticipation of calling her baby Li'l Bit. She was a good girl.

Desiree and I decorated Bitsy's stall, painting the walls light blue with a glad sun and—you guessed it—clouds. We made sure Bit had a clear path to the pasture, and I told her she could eat as much as she wanted, especially since she had a little cow on the way.

Mabel was generous with her land, too. She gave me a plot near the tire swing. It was mine to use, she said, "now and forever." I started my own garden with seedlings Mabel gave me, filling it with flowers and foods, both.

Besides teaching yoga classes, Desiree and I did our best

to get me ready for seventh-grade math, reading, and science. I think we both knew it was fairly futile. There just wasn't enough time. But I loved her for trying.

One day, though, it was just me at Crispy Acres. I had plans to hang a horseshoe over Bitsy's stall. For good luck with her calving, you know? The horseshoe, of course, came from Desiree. The hammer I borrowed—as in they *loaned* it, not I *stole* it—from the Orrs. As I hammered, the heifer watched me, chewing her cud all the while.

I told her all about how Mabel was so brave having her own baby, and I was sure Bit would do just fine, too.

"And I won't ever take your baby from you. That's a promise."

Nearby, someone cleared their throat. I looked up to see a man in overalls, bald in front, but with a long ponytail in the back. His face looked a lot like Crispy's, though, so I figured he was the son who had inherited the Acres.

"Hello," I said.

He jutted his chin at the stall. "You've made her a real nice home here, Miss Cantrell."

"Thanks," I answered. "You can call me Hush. Most people do."

"Glad to meet you, Hush. I'm Jack."

I got up, dusted off my hands, and shook with him. "It's a pleasure, sir. I liked your daddy very much."

He smiled. "Me too." After a few quiet seconds, he said, "My wife, Amy, made some lemonade. She thought you might like a glass."

That sounded good, except, "What I could really use is a pee break. Do you have a bathroom? I'd be glad for some lemonade, after."

He said that would be fine. I patted Bitsy on the nose and promised I'd be back soon. Then Jack and I strolled across Crispy's peaceful acreage and down to the house.

Amy greeted us at the door. "You're always welcome here, Hush. Anytime you're tending your cow, you just come up for a glass of lemonade, or a tinkle, or just to say hi."

I thanked her and managed not to crack a grin about the idea of having a *tinkle*.

Jack pointed me to the bathroom.

I shut the door behind me, remembering the day I'd stolen a box of floss from the Orrs' cabinet. It was nice—and a little peculiar—to be in a stranger's house and not have my loco bearing down on me.

After I did my business, I went to wash up—and found myself face to face with the bathroom mirror.

There was me.

And there were my imps.

I had a lot of them, mostly over my heart. Strangely, a couple clung to the left side of my head. All but a few were pale red. As for those darker ones, I reckoned I knew what they signified.

With a certainty, one imp was my pain at having to leave Mabel's. She was the finest, strongest grown woman I'd ever known, and it was breaking my heart to part from her. And, yeah, I knew I was gonna see her nearly every day, even after summer. She'd even made me her official garden assistant with a name badge and a wage and everything. But it wouldn't be just her and me. We were both package deals now. Mabel with Shaw and Tom and Travis. And me with Nina.

I figured the second pain imp was all about Nina. I hadn't forgiven her, not all the way. My heart just wasn't big enough yet. And, though it didn't happen every time, there were a *lot* of times that just seeing her face made me think of the terrible thing she'd said in Sass Foods. A mother has a great power to hurt her child, if she chooses, and Nina had left me with wounds that were slow to heal.

The last scarlet imp might be harder to fathom. It's definitely harder to own up to. It was my longing for my old life. As a sneak thief, I might have been lonesome and friendless and ornery, but I was also free. I had adventures. And secrets. There is a certain savor to possessing a secret. In my new, honest world, I had few of them—and none of them juicy.

Looking in that mirror, I couldn't help thinking that I wasn't the only pain lifter in town now. Nina hadn't actually plucked any imps, but she *could*. The walk from Crispy Acres to Brandy's was less than a mile long. It wouldn't be

255

hard to hunt down Nina. In twenty minutes, I could be feeling no pain.

The spirit of Granny Cunningham seemed to rise up in me, though. *Pain is a teacher,* she whispered, *and we should heed it.*

So, in the end, it came to this: I could let my mother pluck my pain—letting us both off the hook, in a way—or I could learn what the hurt had to teach me.

I considered the still-thin but not-so-sickly girl in the mirror. All at once, it struck me that she—I—was alive.

I was a real person. Through the ill and the good.

What the heck, I figured. *Keep the pain. It's back-to-school time anyway.*

There were three items I very nearly left in Bitsy's stall, but decided at the last minute to bring to Nina's, for as long as we were staying there. My weed flower, potted in Mabel's pretty yellow pot, I set on our front stoop. The other things I had tucked in my pocket.

"Nina!" I knocked on the door, even though I had a key. "It's Hush!"

I'd decided to stick with the name Hush, except with Mabel, who I still wanted to call me Belle.

Nina opened the door. She was dressed in her new work getup, a pair of jeans and a Beezer's collared shirt.

"You look smart," I said as I entered.

"I finish up my training today," she told me. "Then I'm all alone on the register. I'm so afraid I'll gaum it up!"

I shrugged. "If you give out too much change, we'll just pay it back. Peggy's fairly understanding."

Nina nodded. "She's giving me a real good employee discount."

At the same instant, though in very different tones, we both said, "Toilet paper!"

Nina gave a nervous laugh. To be kind, I laughed along with her.

"Your room's back here," she told me, leading the way. "I guess you know that by now."

"I ought to. I slept in it for a week's worth of nights," I said, following her.

"But now you're here to stay." She threw the light switch. "Right?"

I started to say, *I reckon so*, but my words caught in my throat. The bedroom was so pink and frilly, it looked more like a fancy cake than a place to sleep. There was a dust ruffle and pillow shams—solid pink lace—plus curtains and a comforter decorated in rainbows and pink-hued clouds. It was ugly as all get-out, but it was the first time, ever, that Nina had gone out of her way to do something nice for me.

I even smiled a little. "You did this?"

"Is it all right?" She looked so hopeful.

"It's fine," I said. And because that didn't seem like enough, I added, "Plus, it matches this." I took Desiree's rainbow rock from my pocket and set it on my new, chiffon-covered desk.

Nina set a fingertip to the stone. "That's pretty enough. And it *does* match, don't it?"

I stood for a time longer, staring at the confection that was my room.

"Well, I don't want to be late," Nina said.

"Right," I replied. "Have a good day."

Then, apparently deciding she had to be a little mother-ish, she added, "What'll you do while I'm gone? Study?"

"School doesn't start till tomorrow," I reminded her. "Today I'm teaching yoga."

"Right, yoga." She bobbed her head. "Maybe I'll come to that class sometime?"

I could see this was hard for her. She didn't know how to open a door into her daughter's life, and she wasn't sure she'd be welcome if she did.

"Sure," I said. Then I tiptoed onto my own limb. "I could even teach you a little tonight, when you get home, if you ain't too tired."

Her grin was as wide as her face.

Standing alone in my decorated room, I didn't know whether to laugh or cry. Plainly, Nina had stood in the thrift store contemplating the bedding choices, thinking, *She's a girl. Girls like pink,* and snatched up every pink thing she could afford. It was tough to judge her too harshly, as she really *was* making an almighty effort. But it was a little painful to admit that the only thing my own ma knew about me was that I was female.

Other thoughts came crashing in, too. More big changes were heading my way, starting tomorrow. Besides the beginning-of-the-middle Desiree had mentioned, there'd be plenty of new beginnings, too. Frightful ones, perhaps. Ashamed as I was to worry about such a childish thing, I couldn't help wondering—*would* the kids still call me Smell Cantrell?

The closer school got—and the more inescapable my new life seemed—the bigger the quiver in my liver.

ALARMED

When my pink alarm clock shrieked the next morning, my loco was barreling high-speed down the track of my mind. Head pounding, belly pukish, I watched helplessly as a parade of things I might steal, and where to find them, marched through my brain.

We ain't done, you and I, the loco seemed to say.

Sick and tired, I slapped a hand down on the alarm, hating that clock with every twist in my gut. *Alarm clocks! School! Homework? Are you addled? I'm Hush Cantrell! I ain't no goody-goody! I'm a sneak thief and a rascal! I'm—*

Oh, Lordy. I'm in trouble.

And there was nothing I could do to stop myself! Heck, I didn't even really have a hankering to try. I wanted to steal! I wanted me a big fat stash full of borrows! I just wasn't strong enough!

You're not alone anymore, though, the Voice reminded me.

All at once and just like that, I knew what do to. I'd known it all along.

My loco steamrolled on, showing me a pair of fancy sewing scissors left out on a neighbor's windowsill. I even dreamed the sensation of their cold metal through the cloth of my clothing, after I'd slipped them into my pocket.

Right beside my rainbow rock.

Shut up, loco, I said. *Things are different now.*

I clenched my fists, took a deep breath—and imagined drawing those scissors from my pocket and setting them back on the windowsill.

Then I stomped barefoot into Nina's room.

"Nina," I said. "Wake up, please."

"Mmwhat?"

"Wake up now. It's time to do some mama's duties."

She sat up and rubbed the sleep from her eyes. "You all right?"

I sat down next to her. Without so much as a *good morning,* I explained about my loco.

"Just because things are tidier now, doesn't mean it's gone," I told her, my voice hard with strain. "I'm gonna need to talk about it sometimes. And it won't always be when it's convenient for you. If you can't handle that, you better say so, quick."

She gave me a nod I could almost believe in. "I can handle it."

"All right, then, here it is."

I talked.

And Nina listened.

And by the time Desiree knocked on our door, ready to walk me to school, the loco was nothing more than a quiet rushing sound—a train in the distance.

MAP

It was a full week before I got around to dealing with that slip of paper I'd been carting around in my jeans pocket. Good thing I don't stay on top of my laundry so good.

You have to put it someplace safe, Desiree had told me. *Then, after a while, take it out and see if your treasures have appeared.*

Standing in my new room, I pulled the page from my pocket and unfolded it real careful-like. It was my treasure map, and I hadn't looked on it for nearly three months. *Two little girls holding hands. A lady grinning peacefully in her sleep. A flying bird. And in big, chunky letters, the words* SHE KNOWS LIFE IS MEANT TO BE MAGICAL.

It was no work of art, but maps aren't made to be admired.

A map shows you the way.

Where you've been. Where you are. Where you're going.

I reckoned my map showed a little of each.

I took out a pushpin and tacked it up on the wall.

Then I grabbed my satchel and swung sideways out the front door. Me and Desiree were meeting at Ham's to do our homework over milk shakes.